ROSES IN AMBER

Also by CE Murphy

The Austen Chronicles
Magic & Manners * Sorcery & Society (forthcoming)

The Heartstrike Chronicles
Atlantis Fallen * Prometheus Bound (forthcoming)
Avalon Rising (forthcoming)

The Walker Papers
Urban Shaman * Winter Moon * Thunderbird Falls
Coyote Dreams * Walking Dead * Demon Hunts
Spirit Dances * Raven Calls * No Dominion
Mountain Echoes * Shaman Rises

& with Faith Hunter
Easy Pickings
A Walker Papers/Skinwalker crossover novella

The Old Races Universe
Heart of Stone * House of Cards * Hands of Flame
Baba Yaga's Daughter
Year of Miracles
Kiss of Angels (forthcoming)

The Worldwalker Duology
Truthseeker * Wayfinder

The Inheritors' Cycle
The Queen's Bastard * The Pretender's Crown

Stone's Throe
A Spirit of the Century Novel

Take A Chance
A graphic novel

Roses in Amber
A Beauty and the Beast story

& writing as Murphy Lawless
Raven Heart

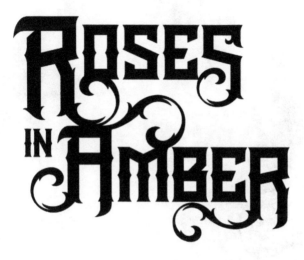

ROSES IN AMBER

A BEAUTY & THE BEAST STORY

C.E. MURPHY

a miz kit production

ROSES IN AMBER
ISBN-13: 978-1-61317-136-3

Cover Artist: Tara O'Shea / fringe-element.net
Editor: Thomas A. Murphy

For Linda Hamilton & Ron Perlman
who taught me to love both my name and poetry

There is a story of a beast, and a merchant's daughter, and a curse that must be broken.

This is not — quite — that story.

I awoke to the acrid scent of smoke. Later I thought that had I not been the youngest, condemned by two older sisters to sleep nearest to the rafters, none of us might have survived. It took two servants and often a dash of cold water to wake my oldest sister on any given morning. Our middle sister woke more easily, but slept so deeply buried in duvets that I already wondered how she did not suffocate. Smoke would have gone unnoticed by both of them until it was too late.

Our brothers, all younger, slept in another

part of the house entirely. They would never have known of the fire until it was far too late for we three sisters, and probably the three of them as well: by the time it reached their wing its strength knew no bounds.

The leaded windows shattered as we ran from the house, glass splintering outward. The children shrieked, especially little Jet, whose first memory might be of the wall of fire reaching toward the night sky. I carried Jasper, whose six years had taught him a great deal about running, but very little about fear, and who had rooted with terror when the flames roared toward us. We all screamed, even Father, when the roof collapsed and threw showers of sparks so high they became indistinguishable from the stars. They came back to earth as sooty streaks, though, raining their darkness on the eight of us. We stood beneath that dark rain, watching helplessly as our wealth melted in rivulets of gold and silver that ran into the gutter, as our account books and library and letters — Maman wrote so many letters! — turned from paper to flame in searing bursts, and as our gowns and suits and jewelry burned and cracked and split.

Father, whose second wife had borne the three boys, stood beside us, clutching Maman's waist to keep her upright as she sobbed uncontrollably. He did not cry; neither could I. Not with the heat drying my throat and stinging my eyes. I wondered, in fact, that

Maman could, but I didn't, at the time, understand her fragility. Or ours, for that matter. Even watching all our possessions burn, I could hardly imagine we would not somehow find ourselves returned to comfort within a few hours. We would find ourselves a comfortable hotel or salon while the house was rebuilt, and look back on the fire as a terrible moment in otherwise pleasant lives. Not too terrible, though. No one had died, not even a servant, making it more of an adventure than a tragedy, and we could dine out on adventure for years.

Flint, the oldest of our brothers, who, at ten years old, came up to my shoulder, wormed his way between myself and Pearl, the eldest of our family. She glanced at him with the expression a dozen or more wealthy suitors had tried to warm into love: irritated affection, directed down the length of a stupendously well-shaped nose. I put my arm around him and he buried his face against me, arms knotted around my middle, as if he performed the role Father did for Maman, but only on the surface. I bent my head to kiss his hair, wondering if it lent any kind of reassurance.

"We'll be fine," said Opal, and if Opal said it, it was difficult to believe it would not be true. Kindness clung to her like a cloak, earnest and gentle and impossible to dissuade. She lifted Jet higher onto her hip, and spoke to him in a reassuringly soft tone. "Amber saved us, and we cannot have been spared for nothing."

"I woke everyone up," I said, all but beneath my breath. "Save for with Pearl, that's hardly a heroic measure."

Flint snorted a laugh against my ribs, and Opal's bright-eyed mirth made a perfect counter to Pearl's withering look. She breathed out once, visible in the darkness, and turned her gaze back to the fire that refused to gutter. That breath made me realize the cold, a cold I had not felt or even imagined, with the flames driving us back another step every few minutes. But of course it was cold: winter had come on us weeks ago, and if there was no snow on the ground tonight, it was only because the inferno that had been our home had melted it all away. The stars beyond the rising sparks had the clarity of cold nights, even through smoke, and beneath my bare feet the cobblestones were slick with water that had recently been ice.

"Jasper." I had put him down once we were past the blaze, but now I called him to me and lifted him into my arms again. His feet, pressed against my night dress, were freezing wet blocks, and, looking down, I saw Flint shifting his weight from one foot to the other, warming the bottom of one on the top of the other. I spoke over his head to Pearl. "We need shoes for the little ones, at least."

She said, "Well, the servants—" and stopped, more flummoxed than I had ever before seen her. Together we children turned to look at our servants, who numbered half again as many as our entire family, and whose bleak faces reflected the red and orange of the flames. Later, I knew that they understood the situation more clearly than we girls did, but in the moment I could only think that for the first time in our lives, our servants were unable to simply step forward with the items necessary to our comfort. All of that fed the fire, and they wore no more shoes or coats than we did.

"The neighbors," I said, without conviction. We *had* neighbors, in the way that any large town estate had them: at a comfortable distance, separated by well-tended gardens and high walls. They were aware of our predicament: I had heard firebells ringing over the fire's thunder, and I was distantly aware that there were groups gathered up and down the street, but none of them had come near us. I looked to my father, whom I supposed should be heading a rescue effort for his childrens' toes, if nothing else, but I saw a man engulfed with his wife's grief, and an uncomfortable thought intruded on my mind.

Had it been one of *our* neighbors whose home was burning, my father would not even go so far as to come out of his own gates to see what the fuss was. He had coached us to mind our own businesses all our lives; other peoples' troubles were for them to deal with. I knew the attitude was born from the false sympathy offered after my birth mother's death: people who had hardly known her, or who had looked down on Father's merchant status, had appeared to shower him with false solicitiousness and to look greedily on his three motherless daughters. In his grief, it was possible he had turned away those whose sympathy had been genuine as well, but the habit of keeping to his—and our—own had been long established before I was old enough to notice it at all.

Still, had our neighbors been in such straits, Opal would have gone anyway, unless Father barred the door to her. She would have gone, carrying blankets and soup and comfort, and I would have followed, because since my memory began, I'd always known that Opal did the right thing for others. Pearl might have been shamed in to coming along by Opal's generosity, but perhaps not. The boys were too young to expect much of, but for the first time in my life, facing a moment of need, I realized that my family had not necessarily won themselves the place in the hearts of others that would compel others to offer a helping hand.

Then a stout woman I vaguely recognized, a cook from one of the homes nearby, came through the smoke with blankets and shoes and an expression of loss greater than my own, and under her mothering wing we were escorted away from the ruins of our lives.

I didn't sleep. The boys puddled around Opal, who, soothed and soothing, drifted into sleep with them. Not even our home burning to the ground could keep Pearl from her own rest; provided with a bed, she returned to slumber before even the boys had. Maman sobbed herself into exhaustion and my father never left her side, so I assumed that he, too, had escaped reality for dreams, but I couldn't. I sat in the window of the bedroom we children had been given, surrounded by a blanket and the wet scent of smoke, and watched until the orange light rising from our burning home was swallowed by the pale blues and pinks of sunrise creeping over the tops of black leafless trees. A hint of icy fog hung in the near distance, but when I went out into it, even the fog had an orange tint, smoke particles clinging to the air.

The smell of smoke was stronger outside, making me realize what I'd smelled inside was my clothes and hair. Remnants of the fire, not its actual strength. I passed through our rescuers' garden, my blanket dragging behind me through thin snow and thicker frost crystals on shards of grass that had not yet succumbed to the snow's weight. A film of ice had coated the street and I was grateful for the ill-fitting shoes I'd been lent as I walked silently toward the smoldering remains of our home.

A tremendous heat still radiated from the ruins, putting paid to any thought I'd had of searching them for surviving trinkets or knick-knacks. Instead I hitched my blanket higher so it wouldn't drag through soot, and paced the perimeter of where the heat-induced melt had reached, venturing closer where I dared. At that distance, the only thing that had survived were the occasional shards of glass, glittering blackly against scorched earth. A flutter began under my heart, wild and frightened, and I dragged in deep breaths of smoky air, trying to quell it. There was no need to be afraid now, when we had all lived through the fire, and I had already known everything we owned had been lost.

Rationality did nothing to calm the rising fear, or to slow my heart. The morning's cold fled beneath my heating blood and I moved faster, faster, until I stumbled at a run around the grounds, searching for anything, *anything* that might offer a link between what we had been, and what we would be. My chest hurt from the effort and the smoke in the cold air, and my eyes burned with tears born from grief and the rising wind.

A brick or a branch or a frozen lump of earth finally brought me to my knees with a wailing thud. I bent forward, fingers scrabbling at blackened earth and forehead pressed against half-thawed soil, and I cried until the ground beneath my face, at least, had softened with tears and mucus. There were brittle, burned branches in the softer soil, all that remained of the roses I'd tended in our garden.

I felt no better at all when I finally lifted my head again. There was no catharsis in sobbing; I didn't feel lighter or emptier or more able to move on. I felt cold, my shins and forearms numb against the ground, and thirsty. I sat up stiffly, wiping my arm across my nose, and gathered myself to stand. Glitters of glass shone against the soot in front of me. In them, a spot of color caught the light. I reached for it, and found, half-buried, a piece of glass the size of my palm. I recognized it instantly as a survivor of the stained glass window in our library. It had looked out over our rose garden, though its height was such the garden couldn't actually be seen through it. Still, it reflected the blooms it had faced: glass roses had spilled rich shades of colored sunlight onto my pages for all the days and months and years I'd spent reading in our library.

Our library was gone.

I closed my hand around the edges of the rose, as if the heavy lead could cut away the ache that suddenly rocked through me, and stared hard at the little piece, trying to will away any more tears. The exterior of the rose was entirely lined in heavy lead, probably explaining its survival: its smaller interior pieces had been protected by the heavy lead, and supported by the finer threads of lead between them. The colors were filthy now, but they would wash, and it was something, at least, from our home.

I rose awkwardly, the glass rose in my hand, and returned to my family.

Father, as tidy as a man could be after a house fire and no bath, was sitting with the rest of the children in our borrowed bedroom, when I returned. I did not often see all of us together, and hesitated in the doorway with a smile despite it all. Father was in his fifties and hearty, with carefully applied color in his hair that left his temples grey and a sense of reliable solidity about him. His features were excellent, deep eyes and a craggy nose set above a patrician mouth and a still-strong jaw. He had fought in the Border Wars as a youth, using his meager pay to buy a ship of his own when the war ended, and as an older man retained most of the broad build he'd developed as a soldier. Age had not yet stooped his shoulders, and his sight remained keen, save for the glasses he wore to read.

Pearl, more awake than I might have expected her at this hour, lounged near him, her own long features a flawless but feminine recreation of his. Her hair lay darker against her shoulders than Father's ever had, a legacy from our birth mother, as was the exceptional paleness of her skin; Father was more sun-touched, though no browner than the sun could make naturally light skin. Opal, still surrounded by the boys, was much prettier than Pearl, but not nearly as beautiful: dark honey-colored hair, tied back in loose waves from a round face with large eyes and rosebud lips, gave her a gentle mothering look that was easier to approach than Pearl's haughty perfection. Suitors thought so, too, and often believed themselves more successful than Pearl's beaus did, because Opal was kind to all of them, and Pearl kind to almost no one.

I lay between them in looks: my hair was closer to Father's in shade, darker than Opal's and lighter than Pearl's. Pearl had Father's nose and mouth; Opal had our dead mother's, and I had an asymmetrical combination of both that earned me the title of *striking*. Men and women both looked on my sisters with pleasure, drinking in their features, but they *studied* me, examining my face as if it was a puzzle to be solved. It had bothered me as a child, but I'd grown to find it amusing, especially when I'd learned I could often take the measure of a person by studying them in return. Most people became guilty and looked away, but a rare few would meet my gaze until we were both smiling, or breathless. Those led to my favorite dances at the balls, and once or twice to more.

The boys, puddled around Opal, all favored Maman in skin tones, sharing some degree of her mahogany coloring. Jet, barely two years old, was darker than she, and still had a baby's bridgeless nose, while Jasper had inherited much of Father's profile and a burnished depth to his skin that set him as destined to grow up as beautiful as Pearl. Flint was closest to Maman in all ways, pretty and delicate and warmly brown, with an artist's hands: he could already play the piano better than I ever would, and I loved to watch him practice. We were an attractive family, and in some way I thought that, as well as our wealth, would protect us from the world.

"Amber." Father extended his hand toward me with a welcoming, but serious, smile. "We wondered where you had gone."

"To the house." I took his hand and sat at his feet, thinking that if Maman was here, that if we were dressed as beautifully as we usually were, that the poses we all now held might have been rendered in oils, a family portrait full of affection and fondness. "There's nothing left. How is Maman?"

Father's expression became even more sombre. "Not well. The fire frightened her. I hope the warmth and safety of a salon will bring her comfort, but, girls," he said, and then, with a fond smile at Flint and Jasper, "*children,* as you boys are old enough to hear household truths now—"

"Some of us are hardly children, Father," Pearl said in her mildest tone, the one that warned most imminently of danger, and Father's smile broadened before falling away.

"No, some of you are not, nor have been for several years now. Still, you are *my* children, regardless of your age. We will not be retiring to the Queen's Corridor, nor to the Grande," he said, naming the two finest hotels in the town. I loved the Corridor, although the queen had never stayed there. It had been built along the road she took after the king died and she went to war to protect our country, and its walls were covered in mosaics that told the story of her victory...and of the loss she faced afterward, when her son the prince had vanished from the earth. She had been young then, and was very, very old now, but her health was reputed to be strong and I half believed the stories that she had sworn her soul to a witch in order to live until the prince's return.

"The Noble, then," Pearl said with a shrug. "Nowhere else could be considered fine enough."

"We will go to the Crossroads," Father said, and all three of us girls caught our breaths. Flint and Jasper, wide-eyed, looked between us, but still did not understand, when Pearl said, "But that's a common *inn*, Father," how far we must have fallen to choose it as our refuge.

"All of our wealth was in the house, Pearl," Father said steadily. "Until the trading ships come in, we must be frugal."

"Frugal?" asked Jasper, and Opal slipped her hand over his shoulder, gentle and reassuring.

"It means we cannot spend money freely. That we must think of necessities, instead of luxuries. Simpler clothing, no new books, plainer meals."

"We will buy fine gowns for you girls," Father said, and in the momentary silence following that surprising remark, understanding fell.

Opal, softly, said, "You mean we are to marry at once."

"You've had many suitors," Father replied. "It will help stabilize our fortunes if you marry now, and well."

"We've had suitors we've turned down," Pearl said. "I'm sure no one will think it desperate at all if we suddenly decide now is the time to wed, particularly if we are to stay somewhere so common as the *Crossroads*, Father. You cannot have it both ways successfully. It is either the Noble," and I noticed that she had, at least, selected the least expensive of the three finest hotels in town, "or spinsters on your hands. Surely our name will give you enough credit to await the ships."

Father took a breath, and Opal's gaze met mine. A knot bound itself in my belly, pressing upward, and I clutched the bit of rose window still in my hand. I did not want to hear what he had to say next, but the words came anyway, relentless with calm. "I'm afraid our credit is already strained, Pearl. The past few seasons have not been as profitable as I might have hoped—"

A gasp parted Pearl's lips, the sound small and sharp enough that she might have taken a blow. Father's jaw rolled, but he continued. "—and our fortunes depend on the incoming ships."

"Why did you not tell us?" Pearl's voice did not rise. She was too cultured for that, but her eyes flashed with fury.

"Because no father wants to tell his children that they verge on destitution, and because we are not so desperate that a good season would not turn it all around. If the next ships had come in with little to show for their journeys, I would have told you then of our situation. The fire has forced me to do so now. I wish it was not so."

"And yet Pearl is right," Opal said in a thin voice. "The house fire is bad enough. If our fortunes are in decline, do we not need a pretense of continuing wealth to ensure good marriages?"

"Beauty rarely requires wealth to come along with it," Father said. "One excellent marriage will offer the other two better chances, and none of you are plain."

"There's no way for us to marry without looking as though we are hastily seeking refuge in another home." I glanced at the rose, hidden in the skirt of my nightdress, then looked back at my father and sisters. "On the other hand, it might seem a perfectly reasonable time for us to do so. It will be months, even years, before our home is reconstructed, and we girls cannot be expected to live in a hotel forever. Society would accept that Father and Maman and the boys might live somewhere more modest for a while, but why would three women of marrying age remain unwed under these circumstances?" I tried to smile, though it felt weak. "You know there are those who say we only stay at home because no one else can match the luxury of our father's house. If he can no longer provide that luxury...."

Pearl examined me as though I had briefly become something new and interesting. Like the puzzle so many others saw me as, perhaps. "I didn't know you could be so mercenary, Amber."

"Well." My smile strengthened. "I do expect *you* to make that first marriage, Pearl. Yours is the ruthless beauty."

She lowered her lashes in a display of modesty that no one who knew her would believe, then brought her gaze to Father again.

"I need at least a month at the Noble to make a marriage, Father. Even I can't do it from the Crossroads."

He looked at her and, though I could see it was against his better judgment, bowed his head. That moment was the first I truly realized my father could not tell his daughters —and perhaps his sons— *no*. We had always teased him about it, but I had never fully believed it, and I did not then understand the price we would all pay for his generosity.

We spent less than a day at our neighbors', and yet the retreat to the Noble came as a relief. Maman joined us, elegant with fragility as Father escorted her from the neighbors' house to the hired coach. I could not begrudge the neighbors for not wanting us, all still stinking of smoke and ash, in their own coach; it would be difficult enough for their servants to air feather mattresses and scrub the smell out of bedclothes. Should it settle into the leather of their carriage, they would carry it with them for months. I did, for the first time in my pampered life, worry a little about the expense, but that was beyond my purview, and if it did not fall out of my head, neither did it keep me from sleeping, as the days went by.

The first day we luxuriated in baths, each of

us girls and father having clean, hot water poured for us, because the filth of soot and smoke blackened the tub so badly with Father's bath that we could not be expected to get clean without new water. The boys had to share a bath, but even they were glad to be rid of the smoke scent, and exhaustion claimed us all as its own that night.

In the morning we were visited by a dressmaker beside herself with concern over our displaced state. We girls received half a dozen new dresses each, with cunning overlays and wraps in different colors that could be switched around to make our wardrobes look thrice the size they were. Maman had three gowns of her own, and Papa two suits; the boys made do with a jacket apiece and two sets of new trousers, tights, blouses, and shoes, the last of which were the quickest in coming, as the cobbler had pre-cut soles ready for the stitching, and we all needed shoes badly.

Most of our servants had been let go, for we had nowhere to house them and no work for a groundskeeper or cook even if we could pay them. Father had his manservant, who helped with the boys, and we four women shared a lady's maid who fussed us into our new gowns and did our hair and made us presentable to the world. Within a week of our house burning, we were comfortable enough at the Noble, taking two rooms for sleeping and a third as our public room, that we might have visitors without being exposed to all the city who came by.

And all the city *did* come by: there was nothing as good as a tragedy to rile peoples' interests. It would have been, by gossips' estimations, vastly superior if someone had died, but there was a breathless interest in us having all survived, as well. Maman had not yet recovered from the shock of it all and played the role of invalid well, while Opal, the gentlest daughter, cared for her in a way that made other mamas imagine she might care well for their own darling sons and grandchildren.

Pearl proved magnificent in adversity, not by denying her aloofness but by playing to it: she sat in the window of our salon, looking shockingly dramatic as she gazed over the city. I didn't believe she had actually lost weight, but rather applied some subtle color to her cheekbones, making them all the more extraordinary. From the street she looked like a princess trapped in a tower. Our first visitors were Maman's closest friends, who went away to witter about Opal's kindness and Pearl's luminescent beauty. (I, being only seventeen, was largely expected to sit quietly, be useful, and eventually take advantage of my older sisters' good marriages.) The words *deathly pale* were heard on the wind, and suitors who had once been spurned now returned to see if the city's legendary beauty was, indeed, at death's door.

"Of course not," Pearl spat bitterly, and turned her face from them with the most delicate tremble, giving the lie—or at least an impression of the lie—to her words.

One of them proposed to her immediately.

Pearl, with more dignity and unspoken wrath than I would be able to conjure in a lifetime, stood and gazed at this unfortunate with a loathing she might usually reserve for a slime eel, or a fungus. "I suppose you ask so that you might have only a little time to put up with me, and a very long time indeed to fondle my fortune. I assure you, sir, I am not that desperate."

She swept from the room at the end of this speech, glancing back only once. But instead of the scathing glance I expected from her, I saw desperation instead. Desperation, vulnerability, hope, trust, and then those emotions were shuttered so fully that I thought I imagined that they had been there at all.

But then I saw the look in her suitors' eyes, and knew that somehow my arrogant sister had convinced them that her coldness was only for show, that she was dying, that she was terrified, and that she would do anything for a show of true passion in her final days.

One of the youths slapped Rafe, who had proposed, along the back of the head, half in jest and in all seriousness. "What were you thinking, man, proposing in front of her entire family? What did you expect her to say?"

Rafe, who was reasonably handsome and extremely wealthy, proved to have an excellent, if sheepish, smile. "She's Pearl Gryce, mate. I expected her to say no. She did before." His gaze lingered on the door Pearl had escaped through, though, before he turned to Father and offered a bow. "May I call again, sir?"

Father, whose eyes had bugged in near apoplexy at Rafe's rejection, made an agreeably non-committal grunt that earned a smile and a bow from Rafe, who then herded his comrades out of our salon to the noisiness of the street. I glanced out from behind the curtain and saw the other youths leaping on Rafe, razzing him and ruffling his hair, but he seemed to take no mind of it, smiling as his own attention returned not to the window I hid in, but the one next door. I imagined Pearl turning swiftly away from that window, a pretense of having been caught, and let the curtain fall as I chuckled. "I didn't know she acted so well."

"Why did she turn him down?" Father demanded.

Even Opal smiled, at that. "Had she accepted, he would have felt himself trapped and found a way out, even with all of us as witnesses. Now it's a chase again, and better yet, a rescue. It's all very romantic."

Better than romantic, it was a horse race:

before evening, one of Rafe's compatriots, a tall youth with a thin mouth and hard eyes returned to ask Father for permission to pay *his* regards to Pearl, and by late the next afternoon two more young gentlemen and an extremely handsome young lady came to admire Pearl's reputedly dying beauty, and made their addresses known.

"Which of them will you accept?" Opal asked that second night, earning Pearl's indifferent shrug.

"Rafe is the wealthiest of them, and unlikely to try to murder me in our bed when I don't conveniently die in a month or two. At least it's easy to appear increasingly fragile, with the quality of food available here." Pearl's nostrils flared just enough to convey absolute contempt, though in fact the Noble's dining hall was fit enough to serve anyone shy of royalty. "I prefer Solindra, though. She has less money but a great deal more charm."

"Solindra Nare has no brothers or sisters," Father said firmly. "Her parents are unlikely to condone a marriage that won't produce an heir."

Pearl rolled her eyes quite magnificently. "Children can be adopted, Father, or a child-maker hired to lie with her if she must be a mother. If we're appallingly canny we might find some young rake with money who'd prefer a husband of his own, and join two more fortunes together for the child's secure future. I'll take another week or two so she doesn't think this is all too easy, and be married before the spring cross-quarter day. I suppose you'll have to come with me, Opal. You can be better presented from Solindra's manor than a hotel, and Amber can move into the Crossroads with Father, if the ships haven't yet come in."

"How thoughtful of you," I said dryly.

Pearl cast me an icy look. "Once Opal is settled she or I will take you in, Amber, but it's easier to marry one woman off at a time. Having all of us hanging about might make someone realize the urgency of the situation."

That, I could not entirely argue with. Neither, in fact, was I in any particular hurry to wed, despite understanding the necessity of it. A little delay orchestrated by my conniving eldest sister was welcome to me.

Rafe, Solindra, and several others called daily for ten afternoons. Each time cold Pearl thawed a little more toward Solindra, who grew more radiant with each of Pearl's smiles, whilst Rafe, who appeared no fool, found himself increasingly attentive of Opal. My middle sister seemed quietly pleased by this turn of events, though I thought Opal would be pleased by anything that helped secure our fortunes. Not because she was a fortune-hunter herself, but because she would worry about us until we were all safe, and think very little of attaching herself to someone pleasant to ensure that safety was engaged. To my amusement, Father became increasingly offended that none of the remaining young men seemed interested in pursuing me, though they were polite enough while trying to steal my sisters' attention. Father began to try to herd them toward me, as if he was a sheepdog and they the sheep—leaving me in a role I dared not contemplate—and I heard them chortling about it on their way out one evening. "Why not?" asked one. "She's got a face you could look at for hours, and none of her older sister's sharpness."

Pearl sent their backs a daggered look indeed: had witchery been more common they might have found themselves bleeding from her glare, but instead the other one shrugged off his reply as the door closed behind them. "Not that one. Why buy the cow when you can have the milk for free?"

I murmured, "Oh dear." My sisters both looked at me, appalled, while Father turned white, then red, and went swiftly into the room he shared with Maman.

Opal said, "Amber?"

"I was very discrete!"

"Apparently not discrete enough." Pearl flung herself into a divan—even that looked graceful on my sister's long frame—and gazed at me with a peculiar mix of horror and admiration. "*Really*, Amber? Who?"

"Well, it hardly matters now, does it? Our

wealthy young friends are still interested in you two, even if I've been, ahm." I glanced toward the door and the departed gossips. "Milked."

"It was that boy at the ball last year, wasn't it? The one who couldn't take his eyes off you. What happened to him? Maybe we can force his hand into marriage."

"For all the stars and the shining moon, Pearl. He left last spring with his parents, to sail for the Eastern Islands and their holdings there. All that gossiping snob who just left has is speculation. People talk because I won't look away when they stare at me. Anyway, if you and Opal have secured good enough marriages and Father's ships come in, either I'll be well enough off that I'm too profitable a union to pass on, or I'll be able to marry someone who doesn't care. Besides," I added with a sly smile, "it was worth it."

A blush crept up Opal's cheeks and she leaned forward to whisper, "Was it? Tell us about it."

My smile became a slow grin, and I bid my sisters nestle closer while I whispered my experiences to them, and we all of us went to bed shyly pleased with ourselves and convinced of our salvation in Solindra Nare's handsome form.

To this day I believe it would have come, had further disaster not struck.

Ships sailed all the year round, but in winter stayed as close to coastlines as they could, the better to hide from storms. We could not expect Father's ships to come in before the equinox, and perhaps not for weeks after that: they had traveled half the world away to the Eastern Islands. They might return laden with silks and gold and ivory, but not until the weather was good enough to risk the open oceans, and the long voyage home.

We could not, then, expect a wretched sailor from a smaller ship to stumble into the Noble's lobby just past the turn of the year, and to fall upon his knees before my father and begin to cry.

Even if the poor man had been more discreet, I suppose it would only have been a matter of hours—perhaps days if we were fortunate, but fortune was not smiling on us of late—before the whole city knew his tale, but as it was, the city learned it nearly as soon as we did.

Father knew the man; even I recognized him as a first mate on one of Father's largest and most prosperous ships, the *Cobweb*. Kneeling at Father's feet, the sailor told his tale.

The trading season in the east had been profoundly successful, so much so that the captain had lifted anchor early and set sail in mid-summer, hoping to arrive home before winter came on too hard. The experienced crew believed they could do it, for all that the journey was often eight months, and, indeed, they had come most of the way when pirates beset them only a few hundred miles from home. Even that had not been quite enough to stop them, but in the wake of the attack, a storm had risen, and men weakened and injured from battle had been unable to hold the line against nature's ferocity. The sailor — his name was Fisher — had been one of four to drag himself into a rowboat as the *Cobweb* and its companions sank, and none of the others had survived the next two days of storms. Fisher had come on foot across half a continent, wretched with grief and ill tidings, and now, looking on him, all I could see was a broken man whose life seemed worthless even to him.

I lifted my eyes to Father, and saw Fisher's fate reflected in his face. I had always thought the conceit of aging in minutes to be only that, a dramatic interpretation, but I saw now that it could happen. He looked heavier, brought farther down than the fire alone could have done, and between one heartbeat and the next I realized we had nothing left to our names at all.

Instead of calling on Pearl as she had done for the past two weeks, that afternoon Solindra Nare sent a polite note begging our forgiveness for her absence, and indicating that she did not know when or if she would once more be able to attend us.

Pearl did not feel the injury of lost love, only the insult of rejection, and drew herself up icy and cold as the sea that had killed the *Cobweb* and its crew. Within a year her dark hair turned pearlescent white, which with her pale green gaze made her presence positively unearthly, but that lay in our future, and we could as of yet barely contemplate our present.

By evening creditors and bankers had darkened our door, calculating the worth of the very dresses we wore, for they were all that we owned, and even they had not yet been paid for. Maman, unable to face their studiously judging expressions, retreated to the room she shared with Father, and for a little while the boys and I joined her. She seemed to take some comfort, especially from the little ones cuddling with her, but when Opal came to enquire after her health, it became clear I was no longer needed. I returned to Father, who sat haggard in a chair in the salon, and could not look at me when I sat beside him.

"Have we anything left at all?" I finally asked.

He shook his head once. "Nothing." Then, instantly contradicting himself, he admitted, "A hunting lodge, far from the city. It belongs to Felicia, solely to her; it was in her father's will that it could not be given to her husband.

It's on none of my records or accounts, although I'm sure someone will make note of it in time, and find a way to take it too, to stack against our debts."

"How, if it is Maman's?"

"Lawyers are good at that sort of thing. Someone will press until the wretched lodge is mentioned, and…" He shrugged, a large and helpless motion.

"Then we must not let them press us."

He chuckled faintly. "You don't know lawyers, Amber. They're relentless. Sharks, save that their skin makes less fine leather. They'll learn about the lodge."

I stood with sudden certainty. "Not if we're not here to press." Father looked at me then, surprised, and I steadied myself with a deep breath. "We must leave the Noble, Father. Tonight. Immediately. I'll trade my gowns for a horse and carriage. We'll take blankets and pillows from the hotel and bundle up, and we'll leave."

"Flee?" Father asked incredulously. "Are you proposing that we *flee*?"

"Do we have another choice? If we stay they'll take the clothes from our backs and the one building we have left to our name. To Maman's name. Solindra won't marry Pearl now, and under slightly more forgiving circumstances Opal's kindness might win her a husband in time, but a wife who has had to live in the streets is too much for any decent man to bear, and nobody was going to marry me any time soon anyway. The boys are too young, even if we could find someone wealthy and generous enough to betroth them to, and we won't, not right now, perhaps not ever. So what choice do we have?"

Father looked at me as though I had become someone else entirely. I almost felt as though I had: running from the only life I'd ever known had certainly not seemed an option half an hour earlier, but then, half an hour earlier I hadn't known there might be one single place for us to run *to*. "I can't run," he said without conviction. "The dishonor...."

"We're already ruined," I said grimly. "How can running make it worse? Go tell Maman and the others to pack what they have, including the hotel's blankets. We'll need them more than the Noble does. I'll get my dresses and..." I faltered. I had barely any idea where to go in daylight hours to acquire a horse and carriage. It was after ten in the evening now, and surely any reputable place would be long-since closed for trade.

"Miss," said an unexpected voice, more gentle and regretful than I had ever heard from him before. I met my father's manservant's eyes, surprised to even see him; servants were simply *not* seen, unless they were necessary, and I hadn't had any idea he was there. "If you'd allow me, Miss, I think I could be of some assistance tonight."

My father burst out, "Glover!" with the same astonishment I felt. His manservant bowed to him, but kept his attention on me. Something happened in that moment, an offering of the mantle, and though I did not fully realize it at the time, I accepted its weight without hesitation.

"I would be grateful, Mr Glover. I'll pack my gowns—"

"If you will allow me, Miss," Glover interrupted, as politely as before, "I believe it would draw less attention if I were to apply a little coin to the situation, rather than half a dozen ladies' gowns."

I hesitated. "There's almost no chance we'll ever be able to repay you, Mr Glover."

"I know." Something else changed in *that* moment, and I almost had the capacity to recognize it: we had become equals, this manservant and I, in a strange meeting of my fall and his rise. I nodded once, but his lean, tall form was already on the move, leaving a polite excuse at the door for his departure.

My father gaped after him, then turned the stupefied expression on me. "What are you doing, girl?"

"I hope to the sun and her sister the moon that I'm saving us all. Go, Father. Pack your things. I think we don't have much time."

I do not know who was more surprised, my father or myself, when, after another moment's silence, he rose to do as he'd been bidden.

The boys were easy: the entire prospect was presented to them as an adventure, and they could hardly contain themselves with excitement about it all. Opal's resistance faded into acceptance so quickly that the former hardly seemed to exist at all, and Pearl, magnificent with rage, acquiesced to the inevitable immediately, if not precisely gracefully.

Maman fainted and would not come to. We packed around her, all of us that much more sombre for her fragility, and if Annalise, our maidservant, didn't help, neither did she hinder us, even when we began to pack the sheets and blankets that belonged to the hotel.

Midnight had come and gone and we had long since finished packing our meager belongings before Glover returned. Jet and Jasper's excitement had not been enough to keep them awake so late, and I collected Jet while Father lifted Jasper's sleeping form into his own arms. Maman, either truly in a desperate faint or in an equally determined one, refused to awaken. Glover, with a glance at Father for permission, picked her up, and it spoke to her sincerity that she did not respond. Pearl, Opal and Flint collected our bags, though there was one too many and Glover said, "If you don't come with us they'll jail you for collusion," to Annalise, who sighed bitterly and took the last bag.

Glover led us out through the servants' stair and halls, our feet treading bare wood that no one of our class had ever walked before, and out a servants' entrance to be met by an enormous, sour-faced nag hitched to a thick, heavy covered wagon. All of us save Glover stopped short in dismay; he climbed with long sure legs over the wagon's tailgate and laid Maman inside before thrusting his head out the bonnet's pinched front. "There was nothing else to be had that would carry ten people. Swiftly, sirs and madams. The watch passes by in another nine minutes, and we do not want to be seen."

Pearl threw her bag in and climbed after with constrained rage. Opal moved more quietly, as if already tired—as well she should be, in the early small hours of the morning—and Glover took Jasper from Father, tucking him into the same small bed on the wagon's floor that Maman was already settled in. Jet was placed between them, and I offered Annalise a hand up. She stared at me sullenly, then took my offer in a fit of pique and flung herself against the back of the wagon as Flint climbed in and Opal tucked blankets around the trio sleeping on the floor.

Father joined Glover at the driver's bench, and their low voices exchanged information for a few minutes before Father, expressionless, joined us in the wagon. Glover, who had not retained a driver — how could he — clambered onto the bench, drew the wagon cover closed as tightly as he could behind him, and clicked to the vast black nag, who lurched into motion with a muttered protest.

I couldn't tell, from inside the snugly covered wagon, what roads he took, only that the cobbles turned quickly to frozen dirt, and that the night watchmen did not hail us. We took blankets from the bags and snuggled together, sleep taking us one by one.

I woke when the wagon stopped just after dawn, and crept through its puckered cover hole to the sounds of the nag slobbering water from a stream. I went a little distance into the wood and squatted to relieve myself, yellow steaming against the snow, then returned to Glover's side. He handed me a tin cup and I scooped from above the horse's watering place, and drank water so cold it made my teeth ache before it slid down to coat my stomach with its chill. I spoke softly, aware of how loud the stream's song was in comparison to the winter morning's silence. "Thank you. You should ride inside for a while. It's freezing."

"And who will drive the wagon?" Glover asked in not-quite-mocking amusement. I gave him a sideways glance, examining his tall, slim form, then gave the nag a better look.

Last night I'd thought her black as pitch. In the dawning light I could see she was a dark bay with black socks, and not a scrap of white anywhere on her. She also stood sixteen hands if she stood an inch, with a belly roughly the size of a barge. Feathery fur grew from her knees down her forelegs and swept magnificently over feet like dinner plates. She rolled an eye at me, and I swear the beast sneered, curling a big lip before puffing a hot breath over the stream and returning to her drink.

I set my jaw. "How hard can it be? If she runs—and surely she won't run, not after walking all night—you'll be right there in the wagon to help rein her in."

"A beauty like this can trot forty miles in a day," Glover said cheerfully. "Plodding along at night isn't enough to wear her out. But I could do with a little warming up," he admitted. "It's a long night, sitting on a bench like that."

I nodded. "Where are we? How far do we have to go?"

"We've come some fifteen miles. It's another seven to the next village—we passed through a couple last night—and we might go on by one or two after that and still be well settled before evening. We can make better time in the light."

Towns and villages lay some seven miles apart by nature, that being the distance most people could walk to a market and get home again in the same day. Even I knew that, though on the occasions we left the city it had always been in a carriage, and seven miles had seemed nothing to me. If we passed through another three villages today, we would be close to fifty miles from the city and that much farther ahead of any pursuit. I found that I preferred, intensely, to be as far away as we could be. "Will she be all right with that much walking?"

"She will," Glover said with confidence. "But an early night will be good for her, after that. We'll rub her down, get her some good oats and some bran, and she'll be set to walk till sundown tomorrow."

"And how far is our journey?"

"Some seventy leagues, miss."

A chill that had nothing to do with the crisp air seized me. I turned involuntarily to look at the road we'd taken already. The last village was well out of sight, not even smoke from chimneys visible above the trees, and those trees closed like dark arches over the lonely frozen road. The gentle blues and pinks of a winter dawn made their frost-rimmed branches beautiful, but not inviting. Like Pearl, I thought, and shivered again as I looked the other way, at the road ahead.

The noisy stream followed the road a little way before diving back down beneath the earth, and the road itself curved gently not too far ahead. Seventy leagues was over two hundred miles, and none of us, save Father, had been more than ten or twenty from our home. Well, perhaps Maman, if the hunting lodge was *hers*, but Maman rarely went beyond the city walls, and certainly we children had never gone so far. I was abruptly afraid, too aware of wolves and boars and bears, all the murderous beasts that lived in the woods. Last night, fleeing had seemed the only sensible thing to do. In dawn's breaking light, knowing there was a week's journey in the winter ahead of us, I wondered if I had been a great fool, condemning my family to starvation in the wilderness.

"Come along, miss," Glover said gently. "When there's nothing left behind you, the only way through is forward. I'll drive with you a bit, and then if big Beauty here doesn't take advantage of you, I'll slip inside for an hour or two's warmth before spelling you again."

"Thank you, Glover." He helped me to the wagon's bench, and under the sun's bright reflective gaze, I learned how to drive a wagon and one, the first of many strange lessons to come.

I hadn't known, until a day of it had gone by, how tired the body could be left from riding in a wagon. I ached everywhere, my limbs were stiff, and my head seemed to bump of its own accord, even when the wagon had stopped. And I was young, and so comparatively unaffected: Father moved like an old man, creaking and grimacing as he stretched. The boys were hardly bothered, leaping about when we stopped and sometimes running alongside the wagon, even in the cold, for an hour or more. After the first day, I joined them as often as I could, and Opal emerged whenever she thought Maman could be left alone for a while. Maman and Annalise refused to leave the wagon except to do the necessary, but once in a while even Pearl stalked along beside the wagon to stretch her legs.

She would not, though, deign to touch the reins. Opal did, with shy amusement, and Flint took them with obvious pride. Even Jasper had a go, and Jet, sitting in Father's lap, held their tails while chattering to birds and rabbits. Mostly, though, Father, Glover and I took turns driving, while Flint walked beside Beauty — for so the big nag had been deemed — at her head, talking softly to her and, as far as I could tell, transforming her personality from surly to soft.

Four days along the road, at lunchtime, Annalise exited the wagon with her chin high and fierce color in her cheeks. "My home village is two miles down that track," she announced. "I'm going back there. I won't go with you to the ends of the earth. I've done nothing wrong and won't serve you in isolation when I've family and friends at home."

Maman let out a terrible cry that affected Annalise not at all as she turned and simply walked away from us. Opal gazed after the girl in pure astonishment, while Pearl's beautiful features pinched with disbelief. I was only surprised because I hadn't known she had somewhere to go; it had been clear she didn't want to be with us. "We have no way to pay her," I said to the cold afternoon air. "There's no reason for her to stay."

Maman cried out again, sending Father and Opal into the wagon to tend to her. Pearl and I exchanged glances before she said, coolly, "There will be more food for the rest of us, then," and climbed into the wagon as well. The boys, standing in a circle of surprise, looked between Glover and myself, and after Annalise, and then Glover said, "We might as well be on the way, then. No sense in losing daylight."

"Will she be all right, walking home from here?"

Glover shook his head. "We've seen no brigands and she seems to know the territory, so I can only assume so. I've a quick step, miss, but I can't walk her home and catch up with Beauty's pace while it's still light out."

"No, I..." I looked after Annalise a moment longer, watching her cloak mottle and fade with distance, and spread my hands. "No, you can't, and she didn't ask. I hope she'll be all right."

"That one lands on her feet." Glover lifted Jet into the back of the wagon. "All right, lads, let's move along."

Flint took up his place at Beauty's head, and we moved along. Barely an hour later, for the first time, we saw a boar on the road: a massive thick-shouldered beast with small eyes and long tusks. Beauty stopped dead and lowered her head, steam puffing from her nostrils as Flint slowly backed up to the wagon's bench. The boar snorted and glared at us while my heart pounded increasingly hard. Surely even a boar understood that Beauty herself was twice his height and ten times his weight, and that without the wagon's cover rising up behind her to treble her apparent size.

But then I remembered that boar hunting was done by groups of men on horseback, often with dogs, and that the boar did not always lose, despite those odds, and I reconsidered what a boar might or might not understand.

Beauty took one solid step forward, leaning her weight into her leading leg, and the boar, with another snort, turned and trotted away into the woods. Glover, at my side on the wagon bench, let go a sharp sigh of relief, and Flint's voice skirrled high with excitement. "Did you see it, Amber? Did you *see* it? It was bigger than I am! Do you think it would have stomped us all? Oh, but if we could have killed it we would have had boar for supper! Wouldn't that have been delicious?"

Glover chuckled and ruffled Flint's hair, a vastly more familiar gesture than he would have allowed himself a week ago. "Yes, lad, but we lack every single weapon we would need to slay such a beast. Had we tried, we would have been *its* supper, not the other way around."

"Boars don't eat people," Flint said stoutly, but he climbed onto the bench with Glover and myself anyway, and kept a wary eye out on the road until darkness fell.

I didn't need to have traveled regularly to know how fortunate we were in the weather. It remained clear the entirety of our journey, the roads staying frozen and easily passed. Clouds followed us on the retreating horizon, thick and grey and threatening snow, but they never caught us. I imagined they might have caught anyone who might pursue us, though, even as I wondered if anyone *had*. None of us spoke of the possibility; what conversation we had centered around Maman's health, which remained fragile, and how we might barter for food or drink at the next village. We scavenged more than one of our dresses, but left the boys' clothes alone, as they had fewer to begin with. We drove past farms and through villages, but mostly we were alone in the forest, until it began to seem the world was nothing *but* forest.

Each morning Father had a low discussion with Glover, who then drove us onward as if he knew the way well. The trees grew thicker and the road narrower, until on the eighth afternoon we passed through a village almost too small for the name, and up an ill-kept track that might once have been a road, and finally through low stone gates to a stone building two stories tall, with a peaked slate roof and windows whose sliding shutters remained tightly sealed. Beauty thudded to a halt and dropped her head to nose at ankle-deep snow. The family slowly climbed out of the wagon to stare at the building, myself with a numb disbelief that seemed reflected in the others. It was not dismay at the small size or condition of the lodge — after weeks in the hotel and then nine days in the wagon, two stories seemed absurdly luxurious to me, who had only a month ago had a room and a library of her own — but rather an inability to fully believe we had arrived.

"The door," Opal finally said. "Is there a key to the door? Maman?"

As if her question had shaken us of a stupor, we began to move again: the boys let go unearthly shrieks and ran through the snow, shouting as they explored. Here were outbuildings; there, a stable with three boxes and room for the wagon. A barn with still-standing fences around it lay some distance off from the main building, and at the back of the lodge, a patch of smooth land that Jasper declared a garden.

Before they were done looking around, Maman had produced a key, which was the most participatory action she had taken in over a week. Glover opened the door onto a single large room dominated by ghostly, sheet-covered furniture and, at one end, a fireplace broad enough for Jasper to lie down in.

A door stood on one side of the fireplace, and on the other, a staircase spiraled upward. The main room was floored with boards as wide across as Jet was tall, and oak beams, aged with time and smoke, stretched heavily across the ceiling, supporting the upper floor. Father opened the inner shutters, then worked stiff iron casings to open the outer ones, and suddenly, despite the late hour of a winter afternoon, the lodge seemed flooded with light. Opal gave a gasp that I thought represented all of our sentiments well, and we turned smiles of real joy and relief upon one another for the first time in weeks.

"Our first business will be making sure that chimney is clear enough for a fire," Glover said briskly. "Where's our lad Flint? He should be of a size to go up it."

Flint, when presented with this prospect, paled enough to turn his umber skin yellow, but Jasper would have been halfway up the flue before anyone blinked, had Glover not collared him with a warning about his clothes. Jasper looked in dismay at himself, then at the manservant. "But I haven't got any others!"

"There may well be something about that we can use," Glover said. "The house was well-sealed up and perhaps they left some necessities of that nature. Go on, upstairs with you to see if there's anything packed away." He gave the order naturally, but I saw it was followed by a certain way of carefully *not* looking at my father, who perhaps ought to have been the one making such suggestions.

Father, though, appeared not to notice. His attention was for the lodge, and I thought he looked better in the minutes since we'd arrived at the lodge than he had in weeks. He guided Maman to a chair without uncovering it, and held her hand as she looked around the lodge. "I haven't been here since I was a child," she finally said. "It looks smaller."

"You're taller," Father said with a smile. Jasper, upstairs, gave a yell of delight, and with eyebrows arched in amusement, I followed him.

To my *own* delight, the stairs spiraled downward as well. "There's a cellar! Maman, this is magnificent!" A few steps upward, I realized the stairs went much higher than the first floor accounted for, and echoed Jasper's shout. "Maman, a loft! Father, there's a floor and two-thirds up here! The roof space isn't wasted!"

"Excellent," Pearl said from below. "You may sleep in the loft, and warn us of fires."

I shot her a sour look equal to one of her own, and finished climbing to the first floor. Jasper had already opened the window shutters and was nursing a pinched thumb for his efforts, but the upstairs rooms were light enough to see a large, well-made bedframe tucked beneath the loft and chests snugged against the opposite wall. I climbed into the loft, which had two small garretted windows of its own, and which was just tall enough at its peak for me to stand up in. Pearl and Father would knock their heads on the oak beams, but the boys would have plenty of room, once something was done about beds. My heart beat faster than the climb accounted for: excitement, even joy, ran through me. This was so much better than I had anticipated that even its isolation couldn't deflate my mood.

"What about these, Amber?" Jasper waved a pair of trousers and a shirt obviously too large for him at me hopefully. I came back down to the first floor and tried them against him, then nodded.

"With a kerchief to cover your hair and face, because I don't know when we'll be able to have a bath and we must keep you as clean as we can. You're a brave boy, Jasper."

He said, "Hnh," dismissively. "It's just a chimney. I'd rather climb that than try to charm Beauty!" He changed clothes, dancing in the chill, then ran downstairs to display himself to Glover and get instructions for cleaning a chimney. Opal, having gone to explore the door beside the fireplace, returned with a broom, and Glover suggested that despite the cold we should go outside while the chimney was cleaned, to prevent soot getting all over us. He stayed to supervise Jasper, and with Flint's help I got both Beauty and the wagon into the stables before unhitching the nag and getting her some of our dwindling grain supplies.

Like the house, the stables had been exceptionally well constructed, and despite their long period of disuse, were in excellent condition. There were cracks to fill and a corner of roof to repair, but nothing that wouldn't keep a while. "I hope the barn is this well kept."

"Jasper and I couldn't get the door open," Flint admitted. "The bar and lock were too tight. But there's wood in the shed and most of it looked dry."

I hugged my little brother. "I think we've landed on our feet, Flint. How lucky we are."

"Have we?" he asked with more wisdom than I would have shown at ten. "Do any of us know how to make bread? Or raise chickens?

Or what to trade for chickens, since we haven't any money left?" His brown eyes suddenly filled with tears. "All we have that's worth anything is Beauty, and I don't want to trade her."

"Neither do I." I hugged him again, then set him back with my hands on his shoulders. "We'll learn to bake bread and do all those things we need to do, Flint. We'll make it work somehow."

A sooty apparition arrived at the stables door, smiling broadly. "I did it!" The smile collapsed. "Maman says I have to wash in snow because I'm too filthy to be let in the house. Opal is cleaning up the mess I made. She borrowed one of the dresses in the chests because nothing she has is practical enough. She looks funny."

"*She* looks funny? Come on, cinder-boy. A snow bath will find my brother under all that soot."

I didn't envy Jasper his bath: *my* hands were red and chapped before we'd finished snow-scrubbing him, and far more of his tender body had to be administered to in order to proclaim him something like clean. By the time we were finished, though, Opal had swept and wiped down the lodge's main room, and Glover had a small fire building in the hearth. We came in shivering to find the sheets had been removed from the furniture, and I stopped just inside the door, staring at ivory and fur lining the chairs and sofas, and the now-revealed mounted heads of animals on the walls. "I didn't know it was possible to use antlers in all of one's decorating."

"Not all of it," Opal called from upstairs. "The bed here is unscathed."

"An oversight, I'm sure!" I shouted back as Father came from the cellar with a tightly rolled bundle that proved to be an enormous brown bearskin rug to warm the floor with. Maman had located—or someone had located for her—a fox-fur muff and hat, and she sat in one of the furry chairs near the fire, watching the little flames as though they were all that kept her alive. Glover came from the kitchen—for that was what lay beyond the door to the left of the hearth—with a dinner of thin soup and bread, making the last of what food we had stretch, and we fell upon it with appetites worthy of the greatest feast.

Afterward, Flint and I dragged the straw mattresses and seat cushions in from the wagon for makeshift beds, while Pearl, who had too much pride to remain useless, and— like the rest of us—too little skill in anything to be useful, went into the cellar and returned minutes later with another, smaller black bearskin rug, which she brought up to the loft. It would do for the little boys to sleep on tonight, at least, and we would begin anew tomorrow.

We would never have survived the next weeks — the next months — without Glover's assistance. The morning after we arrived at the lodge, we girls gave him, with varying degrees of reluctance, all but one each of the fine dresses we had left; the lodge had plainer wear that was scratchy and ill-fitting, but much more practical for everyday working life. He took the gowns and left in the wagon, returning just before sundown with a tremendous variety of materials packed neatly into the wagon.

Among them, inconceivably, were books. Most were practical: books of cooking and building, books about gardening and animal husbandry. A few, though, were for pleasure, and Glover would only look pleased with himself when I turned, speechless with gratitude, to try to thank him. I hung the little stained glass rose in a downstairs window, eliciting gasps from the family, who had not known of its survival, and though every day was long and tiring, I spent a few minutes at the end of each sitting beneath the rose and reading a little bit of a story to my weary family.

Opal learned to make bread from the flour; Pearl, her mouth flat and her hair visibly whitening at the root, proved to be adept at sewing more than just beads onto dresses, and made our homespun clothes fit better. Father took up hunting with the guns that had been stored in the barn, and Jasper went with him while Maman cared for Jet, who loved the hunting lodge and its grounds more than any of us had ever loved our home in the city. Flint, given goats and chickens to master, was rarely indoors again. I joined him outside, learning to break the earth and plant seeds as spring came on. One afternoon, elbow-deep in mulch, I sat back on my heels to look at him, hoeing elsewhere in our garden, and spoke to Glover as he passed by. "Glover, you were a manservant. How on earth did you learn all of these practical skills?"

"I wasn't born dressing gentlemen," he said in amusement. "I grew up on a farm outside the city, but I didn't want to farm. I wanted to live in a fine large house, so I learned to read and to speak well, and began as a footman before becoming a manservant."

"And now you're farming," I said in dismay.

"There's a world of difference when you've chosen to, Miss, rather than it being your unexamined fate. Mind the centipede, Miss, that it doesn't bite you."

I slapped the nasty little beast away, and, contemplative, returned to my mulching.

Glover brought us into the small village

when we would not have gone on our own. Opal, with her pretty face and her open smile, was welcomed instantly, making friends and no few swains, though most of her would-be lovers were already married and — once or twice — already widowed. Pearl's beauty wasn't enough to overcome village reticence, not with her natural arrogance and her now two-toned hair, as inches of it had gone white before we were willing to venture into town. People looked at me as they always had, as if they couldn't help themselves, and as if they might find answers in my asymmetrical features. Flint's way with animals was rumored ahead of him, and Jasper's charm made him a place in the village, as did Jet's childish enthusiasm. Maman remained apart, but the villagers accepted that without question: her people had owned the lodge, and so it was not, it seemed, to be expected that she should mingle.

Father's hunting ability, though, and his permission to hunt the lands, would have made us popular even if we had all been blighted with the pox. He brought in venison for trade twice a month, and smaller game more often: rabbits, pheasants, partridges, even fat squirrels, and the opportunity for meat won the villagers over.

"But they live surrounded by this forest," I breathed to Glover once. "Why do they not hunt?"

"The lands aren't theirs," he replied, "and they're afraid."

"Of what? Maman's family are absentee landlords, at best. It's been decades since anyone has lived at or hunted from the lodge. What could possibly keep them away from the hunt?"

"There are rumors of a beast in the forest, Miss. One who protects it from anyone who lacks the right to hunt."

"Beasts," I said with an unladylike snort, "can't tell who does and who doesn't have the right to hunt."

"And yet the villagers believe." Glover smiled at me, and went to help Father parcel up rabbit in exchange for a length of nicely woven wool.

As summer wore on, my hair lightened to match my name; Opal's became bright with sunshine, and, by the summer cross-quarter day, Pearl took a scissors to her own hair and hacked off the sable length of it, leaving white flyaway curls, when it had been straight before. I watched her do it and was still stunned at the transformation from a prematurely greying beauty to an unearthly creature whose hair and skin seemed equally pale. Her green eyes were terrifying in the midst of whiteness, and she made no effort to tame her alien aspect.

Unexpectedly, the villagers became easier with her after that, as if she had been denying something they all felt was obvious, and now that she had accepted it she could belong. It wasn't long before I realized one or two of them would always approach her when we came into the village, drawing her to the side and murmuring a question. She almost never smiled when asked, but she would go away with them and come back a while later, looking serenely satisfied, which was not an expression I was much used to on my oldest sister's face. One young woman named Lucy, who was lush of form and frank of tongue, called Pearl away often, and after a few weeks I could stand it no longer. I cornered my older sister when we arrived home, demanding, "What do they ask you?"

Pearl's eyebrows had gone white, too, and they rose a little. "For blessings, mostly. On their children, or their pregnancies, or the crops."

"Why on earth would they do that?"

"They think I'm a witch."

I stared at her. "Are you?"

"Maybe," Pearl said, and would say no more.

The harvest season meant harder work than any of us—save perhaps Glover—had ever known in our lives. Opal and Father bore it stoically and Pearl, ill-temperedly, while the boys complained without surcease and yet did their fair share of the work.

I loved it. I had no idea why, but I did: the relentless effort of bending and picking and digging and packing felt wonderful. I learned to make jam from wild berries, puckering my mouth when they were tart and wondering if we might grow sugar beets with any success over the next season. The jams and parsnips and carrots and dried meats went into the cellar, where it remained cool all the year around, and before winter came on we picked apples and pears from the trees that had proven to bear them. I pickled tomatoes and sweated over rose hip jelly, stored beans and traded for spices, and, remembering my sisters' love of perfumes back when we could afford such things, delved into one of the books Glover had brought. There I found recipes for rose water and amber toilets. I conspired with Glover, who brought me vials for the perfumes, and I brewed them in the barn, where my sisters rarely went. The boys, who often ventured there, were sworn to secrecy, and, as they clearly had secrets of their own, did a fair job of keeping them.

I was leaving the barn one afternoon just before the winter equinox when I caught a glimpse of Glover standing unusually idle in the garden. We had turned the soil over already, leaving it ready for next spring's planting, and there was little enough left to be done there. Curious, I went to hail him, then saw that from where he stood, he could gaze unimpeded through the rose window in the house, yet barely be seen from indoors. I knew without error where his attention lay: on Opal, who had set a small loom near the window, and was learning the craft.

His expression was not fatuous, but soft, and I suddenly understood why my father's manservant had been willing to help us, uncompensated, for all these months. I doubted, even then, that he intended to put himself forward: Opal, being the woman she was, would marry him out of gratitude for what he'd done for us, and his was not the face of a man who wished to be rewarded unless his lover's sentiment was as strong as his own.

And still, what a strange gift it must have seemed to him, for our family to fall on hard times that he could help us through. In the city, Opal would have remained impossibly far above his station. I wasn't proud of having often not even noticed our servants, but that I had not remained fact. At least in the world as it had become, he could earn her notice, even her friendship, which was more than he might ever have expected before. He was not *so* much older than she: not yet thirty, I thought, and Opal was approaching her twenty-first birthday now, after nearly a year in the lodge. The difference between Maman and Father's age was considerably greater; Maman was, I believed, barely ten years Pearl's elder, although her constant fragility made me think of her as much older. Opal could do much worse than Glover, and in a village of men either already married or not yet bearded, probably would.

I stepped back and opened the barn door again so I could close it with more vigor, its thump alerting Glover to my presence. He returned to the work he'd been pursuing — fetching wood for the fire, as it turned out — and I helped, taking a load almost as heavy as his into the lodge.

The main room was warmest, of course, and we spent most of what I advisedly thought of as our idle time in it. In truth we had vastly less idle time than we once had, and it was rarely idle at all, as evidenced by Opal's weaving and Maman's stitching, and — surprisingly — by Pearl's pouring over a book I was unfamiliar with. Father held a knife and a long piece of wood in his strong hands, pare by pare creating a board for a bedframe that would in time go into the loft, and Flint sat by the fire bent over a piece of leather that began to look like a bridle. Jasper lay on the bearskin rug with Jet and a piece of slate and chalk, practicing letters with the little one, and as Glover placed another log on the fire, an overwhelming brightness filled my eyes and chest.

"Look at us." My voice cracked and I

swallowed, smiling through a tightness in my throat. Pearl looked up, white eyebrows elevated, but rolled her eyes in disdain as I continued. "Look at us. When do you last remember, in the city, us all being in a single room together, bent to our individual interests but still a family?"

Glover took a discreet step backward, toward the shadow of the kitchen door, clearly dismissing himself as part of the picture I saw, but I said, "Don't leave, Glover. You've become part of this family too. An integral part, I dare say. We would never have made it this far without you."

"Miss," Glover protested, but he smiled, and ducked his head when Opal smiled her agreement toward him.

"We've done well," I insisted. "I don't know that I would go back to what we had, even if I could."

"I would," Pearl said dryly, but Father gave me an odd, approving smile while Maman kept her attention fiercely on her stitching. The boys were entirely unmoved by my emotion, and as such, caused me to release it in a quick laugh. I went happy to my next task, and if I imagined Opal's gaze lingering thoughtfully on Glover for a few moments, I enjoyed that little dream as well.

The longest night came on us only a few days later, and I, expecting nothing, brought out the perfumes for my sisters and Maman, and new winter boots that I'd traded other vials of perfume for, for all the menfolk, including Glover, whose visible surprise was worth having snuck around the village behind his back. Then Maman, who had spent nearly a year in almost absolute silence, rose and went upstairs, only to return with warm and beautifully stitched cloaks for all of us, even—as I had done—Glover.

More gifts: sleds for the little boys from Father, leather-worked pendants of our favorite animals—or in my case, of a rose, a reminder of the garden that had burned—from Flint, warm dresses and new shirts all around from Opal, who said, "Next year I'll have woven the fabric, too," almost defiantly. Glover had pretty things for each of us girls, which I thought covered the excuse to give Opal a necklace *of* opal, the pendant gleaming with depth, and for the boys, hand-carved horses and a carriage whose wheels turned smoothly.

Pearl produced a deck of witch's cards that I was certain she hadn't owned a year ago, and played at reading our fortunes. I believed only I caught the downturn of her mouth a few times as she pulled cards from the deck, or the sharp glances she bestowed on Maman, Father, and myself. But she offered nothing in her readings beyond laughter and good fortune, and then to our delight Jasper and Jet stood up together and first recited the Winter Enchantment, an ancient poem to bring back the sun, then sang for us the first of many solstice carols, inviting us to join them in the next as they finished the first. We nursed the hearthfire, adhering, as we hadn't done in the city, to the old tradition of lighting no new fires on the solstice for fear of angering the faeries and spirits, and we placed a candle in the eastern window, to guide the sun back home again.

The boys gradually drifted into sleep, but—again, as we had not done in the city—we adults remained awake, growing increasingly quiet as the night went on, and awaited the return of light to a world that had, at this time a year ago, seemed impossibly dark.

A traveler arrived with the returning sun.

I pretended for a moment that he had come to the village the night before, and stayed there until daylight broke again, but his face was ruddy with cold, snot dripping from his nose and frost rimming both his heavily furred hat and his beard. His horse did not look rested, or well-fed, or even warm, though its breath steamed heavily in the winter air.

Father opened the door as the traveler rode up the drive, and I could see from his expression that he knew the man. He stood in the open door, waiting, and the man swung off his horse and said, without preamble, "The

Spidersilk survived."

Maman cried out, but Father's knees cut from under him; had he not held the door frame he would have fallen. It took ten heartbeats before he gathered himself and straightened, then stepped into the house and said, "You'd better come in."

Once inside and divested of coat and hat, I —we all—recognized the man as Captain Stewart, who had sailed the *Spidersilk.* He told much the same story Fisher had almost a year ago, save with the *Spidersilk's* fate being driven hopelessly off-course. The crew had come, essentially by chance, on an island with enough of a harbor for safety, and had waited out the winter storms there. The stars had guided them back toward home, but the poor *Spidersilk* had been so badly damaged that as much time was spent keeping it afloat every day as making headway. Stewart had limped it into port only a few weeks earlier, learned of our misfortunes and our disappearance—still fodder for gossip, it seemed—and, remembering an idle conversation with Father about the hunting lodge years earlier, had set off in search of the family without telling anyone where, exactly, he intended to go.

"The cargo," Father said.

Stewart shook his head. "Not what it was when we set out. Time and weather has taken some toll. Still, silks and spices and gems—"

Pearl made a noise at this, a rough whimper

unlike herself. Opal, almost as pale as Pearl, took her older sister's hand, while Glover, at the kitchen door, twisted half a smile and glanced away. I hadn't yet moved, unable to consider what another reversal of fortune meant. Just days ago I'd proclaimed I wouldn't go back to what we'd had, but then the possibility hadn't existed. In this new light, I was no longer so certain of my convictions.

Maman rose and came to clutch Father's hand while the boys stayed silent, even Jet knowing something important was happening, though he couldn't understand what.

"You'd better come," Stewart finally said. "The goods are yours, and so are the—" He broke off, glancing at the family, and shrugged, though we could all fill in the final word: *debts.*

"Tomorrow," Father said heavily. "You and your horse both need rest, and there's nothing a day's delay will change."

Stewart stayed, and the day took on a shrill edge as Father packed for the journey. The boys were overcome with the idea of innumerable toys again, though Flint insisted loudly and at length that he would have to take the goats and chickens with him. Beauty, of course, was a foregone conclusion: none of us could imagine life without the enormous bay mare anymore. Maman whispered with Opal about silks and fine smalls, and Opal, who had always seemed happy enough, rubbed the callouses on her hands and wondered if they would fade. Glover said nothing, and I watched the proceedings with a conflict of desires. Strangely, so too did Pearl, though she could be drawn into Maman and Opal's talk of beautiful dresses and shoes that were for show rather than sensible.

Our guest was given a hay mattress in front of the fire, and we retired to bed early, all too aware that Father would depart before the midwinter sun rose. I was changing into my nightdress when Pearl appeared, clutching her own nightgown and the new cloak from Maman around her for warmth. "You have to go with him."

"What?" I pulled the nightdress on and, although I'd heard her perfectly clearly, repeated, "What?"

She seized my shoulders, a more physically abrupt gesture than I was accustomed to from my reserved eldest sister, and almost shook me as she said, "You must go with him, Amber." Her green eyes were alight even in the darkness, from which she stood out like an apparition, ghostly and white.

I put my hands on hers at my shoulders, then took them away from that fierce grip and held them instead. "Why?"

Pearl shook her head once. "I don't know, but I saw it in the cards. I saw a journey for Father, and a death."

"Pearl!"

"I told you," Pearl said, although she hadn't, quite. "I'm a witch."

"Pearl," I protested, only half seriously, "if every woman rejected by a lover became a witch, there would be only witches in the world."

My sister's features settled into a reassuringly familiar contemptuous look, and her tone scathed as she said, "Father's cards showed a journey and a death, and Maman's lain beside his warned of secrets told and another death. But when yours crossed theirs, the fortune changed."

"To what?" Despite my protest, I found myself inclined to take Pearl seriously. She had never evidenced much sense of humor, and most women rejected by a lover didn't go white-haired overnight, either. That she had become a witch did not, somehow, seem so far-fetched.

"A journey and a bargain, secrets told and danger faced."

Something in how she stopped warned me. "And?"

Pearl shook her head. "The last card I turned usually means change."

"But?" A cool certainty slid through me, and unusual anguish creased Pearl's lovely features.

"But crossing Father's fortune, it could yet mean death."

I had already known, so it only took my

breath a little. "So if I stay, he dies, and if I go, I might die."

"It might just mean change, Amber…."

"Pearl." I hugged my older sister for the first time that I could remember, then set her back with my hands on *her* shoulders, and said, simply, "Of course I'm going."

The others were not so easily convinced.

I presented it as already done: my bag was packed with much more practical clothes than I'd traveled in a year before, and with vials of the perfumes I'd made, as I was of a mind to sell some. Pearl, who was not guileless, but who had never in her life been bothered to lie, said I had told her the night before that I intended to go with Father, and that she thought a younger person on the road with him was wise.

Flint, now closer to twelve than eleven, proposed that *he* should be the one to go, as he was very nearly the next man in the family. Glover, as an actual adult, looked torn but said nothing, for which I was grateful; my family needed him more than they needed me. Father would have none of it: he could go on his own, with Stewart, and they would be fine. The argument—if everyone else voicing an opinion while I remained silently steadfast in mine could be called an argument—went on for some while, until the sun threatened the horizon, upon which I said, "We'll be losing daylight soon. If you don't take me with you, I'll walk along behind."

I saw Father take in the possibility of restraining me, mostly with a glance at Glover, and, as quickly, reject the thought. I could not be kept tied up for weeks, and he concluded, correctly, that once I was released no one would prevent me from walking alone to the city, a journey vastly more dangerous on my own than with them. He said, "Very well," and in no more than another twenty minutes, Beauty was hitched to the wagon, which had its cover tightly drawn, Stewart's horse was tied to the tailgate, and we were on our way.

I soon learned that riding alone was vastly colder than riding in a wagon bundled with eight or nine other people, but considerably faster. To stave off both boredom and cold, I walked often, though I could not keep up with Beauty's less-laden pace as easily as I'd walked with her a year ago. On the other hand, I could walk much farther and faster than I did a year ago, and found a certain joy in pushing myself to keep up with the big horse. Stewart, who seemed to regard me as confounding and perhaps alarming, came around to my determination by the end of our journey, and joshed with me as easily as he might have one of his men. I was sorry to have the city's profile come into sight, and shocked, as we entered its gates, to realize that its sounds and smells, which had once been an unobserved backdrop to my life, were now unpleasantly loud and profound to me.

Stewart, watching my face, released a sympathetic chuckle. "I feel that way every time I come back from the sea, lass. After this past year, the worst sail of my life, I swore I'd never set foot on a ship again, but half an hour in town made me reconsider it all, despite everything."

"There are so many people," I said, a little wonderingly. They had a method to them, streams of passers-by going one way or another, but eddies and stops were created by sudden encounters, and the whole of the pattern had to shift and accommodate those changes. Children disrupted it all, going where they wanted, and voices, bells, wheels, beasts, all came together to create a cacophony that made my skin twitch. We passed through the chaos to the Crossroads, that inn which a year ago had not been good enough for my sister Pearl, and took two rooms that Father paid for with coin earned from his hunting.

We bathed that night, me in my room and the men in theirs, and in the morning, dressed as well as we could be, we went first to the docks to see the *Spidersilk* and its crew, and then, having assessed the cargo, Father went grimly to the bank.

Left to myself, I could have—perhaps

should have — returned to the inn to wait like a dutiful daughter. Instead, thinking of the people I *knew* we owed money to, I went to the dressmaker whose sympathy had clothed us after the fire, and offered her eight vials of perfume as payment.

A wonderful combination of scorn and greed lit her eyes when I made the offer: in the city commerce was done with cash, not trade. But perfume was expensive, and mine was exquisitely scented, with a base that warmed to the wearer and made it unique to them. She tipped a drop of one against her wrist to test its scent and inhaled, then did her best to school her expression into disdain. But she took the offer, and with it, information worth more than coin: gossip. The Gryce family had returned, at least in part, and the youngest sister had lowered herself to engage in perfumery and trade. That knowledge would be worth as much as the perfume itself, if not more: people would come for weeks or months to have gowns made by her, just so they could hear in person about my rough hands and country dress.

The Noble, where we'd stolen blankets and pillows, would not be so easily put off. I visited cloakmakers and cobblers, inviting them to the Crossroads to see the furs we'd brought, furs that in our village we could trade for goods, but which in the city would be bought for cash. More than one tradesman leered at me, which they never would have dared to do a year ago, but several sent a journeyman to the inn to inspect our wares anyway. Father had tanned them well, and we had a handsome variety of fox, beaver, and rabbit, and a wolf skin from a solitary beast who'd thought our chickens were for his benefit.

That night it snowed, a thick white blanket muffling the city sounds, and in the morning nearly all of the journeymen returned, ploughing through the snow with their feet. One or two came with their masters, and they all, journeymen and masters alike, made offers on the furs. I sent the unaccompanied journeymen back to their masters with instructions to take me seriously, and by late evening—thanks in part to snow falling incessantly throughout the day, and the potential of a long cold season ahead—they had engaged in bidding wars that drove the prices up as far as the market would bear. The highest buyers left cards with me, asking that I come to them directly if we should return next year with more furs.

On the third morning, cash in hand, I waded through the snow to visit the management of the Noble, and with as much grace as I could present, paid them for our accommodations a year earlier, the materials we'd taken, and added noticeable but not offensively large percentage on top of that to make certain they had no interest in pursuing us toward a debtors prison. The jowly gentleman who ran the establishment looked at the pile of coin and, with business-like sincerity, invited us to stay with them at the Noble at any time in the future.

Everything else was beyond me: I didn't know who Father owed money to, or in what quantities, and could not myself go to make good the debts. The night I paid off the Noble bill, Father returned to the Crossroads to say he had brokered an agreement with the bank and his debtors that we would sell the cargo.

Given that much leeway, I insisted we bring the salt-roughened silks, in equal parts, to the dressmaker who had taken my perfumes, and to the ones we had most often frequented when we lived in the city. As with the perfume, as with the furs, the added value of gossip made them pay more than they might have otherwise, and on top of that, the silk had been through *adventures.* Its roughness could be seen as a fashion statement, and as such, had greater worth still. Furthermore, in only two days and despite the steadily falling snow, the story of my perfume had spread, and the other dressmakers bought vials from me as entirely separate transactions. We left more flush with cash than either of us had expected, and Father, once we were safely back at the Crossroads, looked at me in astonishment.

"If I'd had any idea you could bargain like

that, Amber, I would have brought you into business with me before the troubles began. They might never have happened."

"I don't know that I could bargain like this before our troubles, Father. I learned it in the village, not the city."

Father shook his head and smiled. "The bank was reluctant to let me be the one to sell the cargo, for fear our bad name would taint it. But banks won't drive a hard bargain themselves. They see the money as already lost, and whatever they can get against it is an unexpectedly pleasant offset against the losses. They valued the silk at two thirds of what you've gotten for it, and if you can do that with the jewels...."

I could. The jewels were easier, in a way: salt didn't damage them, and pirates, storms, and having been lost at sea made a magnificent tale for any centerpiece of a necklace or ring. I traded perfume for trinkets for my sisters: a pearl ring for Pearl, and an opal necklace for Opal, and both the jewelers and myself felt we'd come out well. Little by little we paid off debts, until the cargo was gone and even the *Spidersilk*'s remaining crew — a skeleton of what it had once been — had been paid. The evening after we paid them, my father counted what little cash we had left onto a table in our inn rooms, then sat back with the money between himself and me.

"Tell me what you would do, Amber. Send

Stewart and the *Spidersilk* back out? Try to recoup our losses, begin again? Or take what we have and return home a little wealthier, perhaps a little wiser?" His smile had bitter edges, all his mockery directed inward.

I sat across from him, hands steepled against my lips, and considered not only his question, but the other money: the coin from selling my perfumes, and the furs that had brought cash to us free and clear of Father's debts. "It's enough," I said behind my fingers. "Perhaps only just, but it's enough to refurbish the *Spidersilk* and send it out again." I lifted my eyes to his. "Or we could offer the ship to Stewart for a nominal cost, let him take on the repairs and the risk of future ventures, and take what we have home again. I meant what I said at midwinter, Father. We've done well enough, at the lodge, and both my perfumes and your furs will sell if we want to come to the city once a year with them. In autumn, not winter." I cast an eye toward the window. We had been in the city two weeks now, and it had snowed nearly every day. Even Beauty would be slow, pulling the wagon home on roads filled with snow.

"Farming is a hard life," Father said quietly. "Full of new risks every season—"

"Unlike mercantile investment," I said dryly, and he laughed, surprised.

"There is that. But if I could make back our fortune, you girls could marry well. Live a gentler life."

"This," I said with a gesture at our earnings, "is nothing, here. But it *is* a fortune at the lodge, Father. It could buy us a cow and pigs. If we come back with furs and perfumes for a few years, and no further debts to pay here, it could buy Flint horses to breed, and a future for the boys."

"But you girls."

"None of us will be outrageously old in another two or three years, Father. If we've done well and want to come back to the city to find suitors and marry, there will be time yet." I thought, but did not say, *Pearl is a witch, and in the stories, witches never seem to marry*, and I had hopes for Opal and Glover, even if I was the only one sporting them. "I think we're better off without the *Spidersilk*. And," I added, suddenly cheerful, "if the others disagree, in the end, you can blame me. I'm sure Pearl will enjoy eviscerating me."

To my surprise, Father laughed again, and said, ruefully, "Ah, Pearl. It's good she's so beautiful."

"Perhaps if she wasn't she wouldn't be quite so...Pearl-ish."

"But imagine if she was, without the beauty."

"I suppose we would love her anyway."

"But would anyone else?" Father took my hand and squeezed it. "Very well, Amber. I'll heed your advice, and tomorrow, offer the

Spidersilk to Stewart, at whatever cost he can afford. Then as soon as the weather breaks we'll go home. I miss your mother." A furrow creased his forehead, and I breathed a smile.

"Maman is my mother," I said gently. "The only one I've ever known."

Father nodded, but after a moment, said, "I miss your mother, too. You look like her, you know."

I shook my head. "I don't. I've seen paintings. She looked like Opal."

"Paintings flatter where they shouldn't always. Her smile was like yours." He gestured at my mouth, at its slight unevenness and the way it made even my sweetest smile look like a smirk. "A little crooked. The painters gave her more even features, like Opal has, but she looked more like you. Ah, I see her in all of you, though. She was often kind, like Opal, but she could be so haughty and reserved that in comparison Pearl looks like the most approachable of women."

"You never talk about her," I said softly.

"I wasn't good enough for her." Father lifted a hand, stopping my protest, and chuckled. "In truth, I wasn't. I met her during the Border Wars, while she nursed for the army. Her family wouldn't come to the wedding. She said they were furious with me for taking her away from them, and her for marrying me."

"Mother had family?" The idea struck me like a gong, reverberating astonishingly in my mind. "We have other family?"

"Her family were friends of the queen, a long time ago. Felicity knew them, too. She came to make sure you girls were all right, after Eleanor died, and after a while we fell in love." The corner of his mouth pulled up. "Her family were also furious, though she still wrote —writes—to them, and they to her. I've been graced with women who are too good for me, Amber, and that includes you girls. I'm sorry I haven't done better by you."

"The *queen*?" Everything else Father had said fell by the wayside with that revelation. The Queen's War—the one commemorated in the Queen's Corridor mosaics—had been years ago, so many years that the number of decades was foggy in my mind, and half impossible to believe. "Our mother—*Maman*?—knew the *queen*? But the queen is—is—" *Ancient* was the only word that came to mind, and though it was by all appearances true, it still seemed rude to apply to our sovereign.

"I didn't say they were age-mates," Father pointed out. "But yes, Maman, and your birth mother, did both know the queen. And I suppose you do have other family, Amber. I don't know them at all, so it's hard to think of them that way." He pulled at his chin, a gesture that would look better if he'd grown a beard, but he had resolutely kept the city's clean-shaven look, even after a year in the country. "I never thought to contact them," he admitted. "Even at the worst of our travails, I never thought of it. Perhaps I should have. For your sake, Amber. For all of you children."

"Sooner salt the earth and curse the sun," I said, offended. "If they wouldn't have you, they've no right to us."

Father chuckled again, but said, "I wonder if your sisters would feel the same way," before letting it go. "Tomorrow, Amber. We'll talk with Stewart tomorrow, and leave for home as soon as we can."

The weather had broken in the morning: sunlight reflected brightly off banked snow and cast blue shadows in its depths. Father whistled merrily on his way out of the inn, and I, mindful of the stories he'd told the night before, went to visit the mosaics along the Queen's Corridor for the first time since before our house had burned.

The elegant frames told the story of our country's darkest hour, so long ago now that even the children of its war veterans were dead, and their grandchildren old. We had been ruled then by a king thought too gentle to rule well: he preferred diplomacy to warfare, and conceded too much, too often, to those who pressed at our borders. When illness struck him down, our enemies amassed, anticipating an easy conquest of a weak country with only a young queen on its throne.

They were not prepared for Irindala's ferocity. She gave her son, the prince and heir to the throne, to her closest friend to raise safely while she rode to war, and ride she did, with an army of the people at her back. Irindala fought alongside the people, bleeding for her country as they did; the first few panels of the mosaic, depicting the king's death and the gathered enemies, then Irindala leading her army, and finally a bloody battle, had frightened me as a child. The centermost, though, had inspired me then, and, a little to my embarrassment, still did: Irindala tall and strong with light all around her, her sword in one hand and the other open to the people, upon whose uplifted hands she stood, trusting them for her strength and balance. I knew now it was a cunning piece of propaganda, but its affect was no less for knowing that.

The next frame, though, broke my heart. Irindala returned to an empty castle, her trusted friend and her son both gone. In every remaining mosaic, Irindala wore a gown with a red slash across the breast, as she was said to every day, to show that her heart had been cut out and could never heal.

She did not become a cruel mistress, though. Despite her own heartbreak, she ruled fairly, and the next panel was broken into four smaller images, showing critical moments in her reign. The last of those reflected a battle from the Border Wars that Father had fought in, pushing back against an encroaching enemy said to be infused with faery blood, so relentless and powerful were they. But Irindala's army triumphed again, as it, and she, had done all through her long reign, save in the matter of her son.

At the end lay one final open space, where the end of Irindala's story would be told with beads of colored glass and glue, marking the end of an era so extended it already belonged to the stuff of legend, and someday would be thought myth.

I could hardly imagine my father fitting into that story somewhere, his part too small to be seen in a mosaic, but still a part of it, if my birth mother and Maman had both, somehow, known Irindala herself. Nor could I imagine asking Maman about it; she was inclined to vapors over a chicken wandering across the threshold, and I thought asking her about her childhood would induce one of her month-long silences. I tried, briefly, to imagine what kind of life *we* might have had, if our mothers had stayed in contact with their royally-associated families, and my imagination failed me there, too, although the idea made me laugh. We girls, at least, had grown up in luxury. Improving on it would have brought our comfort to unimaginable levels. No one needed that level of indulgence. I had learned, in fact, that no one even needed the kind I had grown up with, although that thought would have once been incomprehensible to me.

I gave the mosaics an unselfconscious curtsy, and went on to the shops to buy a few more gifts—finer fabrics, newer shoes, sweets that would last the journey, and other things—for my family, and was ready to leave when Father returned from selling the *Spidersilk* to Captain Stewart. We wouldn't get far with only an hour or two of daylight left to us, but we were both eager to be on the road home.

Beauty, on the other hand, paused at the stable doors and glowered at us, as if the snow —packing down now, at least—was our fault, and as if a filthy enough look would make us agree to put the journey off until the snow had melted. I patted her jawbone, apologized, led her out to hitch her to the wagon, and we were on our way.

@}-,-`-. ~ .-`-,-{@

Clear, cold weather followed us, the lengthening days letting us eke a little more distance out of each day traveled. We stopped reluctantly the sixth night, knowing ourselves to be within a day's travel of home, but also knowing we were *most* of a day's travel from home, and that we would only exhaust ourselves and Beauty if we pushed onward that night. That was my doing; we had lost half a day's travel when I'd recognized the road our lady's maid, Annalise, had taken to the village she said was her own. Father had not objected aloud when I turned Beauty down the little track, and we had emerged into a healthy village nestled in the woods only a little while later.

We were strangers there, drawing the attention of first children, then parents and grandparents who emerged from warm houses to see what we wanted. I asked for Annalise, and followed the child who ran to fetch her; I did not want to talk to her in front of her entire village. She met me at a doorway near the far end of the village, wrapped in a wool shawl and with anger tightening the lines of her face.

"Our debts are settled in the city," I told her quietly. "I've brought the wages we couldn't pay you a year ago, and if you'd like to return to the city to work, I'll ask Glover to come in the spring and offer you safe escort. Mostly I wanted to say I'm sorry, Annalise. I'm sorry you were pulled down into this with all of us. You deserved better."

Agreement and surprise, still dominated by anger, fluttered across her face. "I did." She took the purse of coin and folded it against her belt, glaring at me. "What work could I find now, after disgracing myself by running away with you? Your references would be of no use to me."

I made a face. "Being the center of gossip got us better prices on some things than we might have expected. Returning to the city as the only intimate witness to our downfall might be enough to find you an excellent place. If you decide you'd like Glover's escort, write to us. We'll do what we can. I am sorry," I said again, then left her alone to make her decisions. The village folk didn't bother waiting until we'd driven away to converge on Annalise's home. I hoped I'd done her some good with the visit, even if it delayed us by a few hours, and left us unable to reach home the night we'd planned to.

"Tomorrow," Father said cheerfully, as we tethered Beauty and tied the wagon cover tight to keep us warm. He had been cheerful since we left the city, as if selling the *Spidersilk* had lifted some last weight from his shoulders, releasing him forever from the mistakes he'd made in the past.

"Tomorrow," I agreed, but we were both wakened in the smallest hours of the morning, not by the sound, but by the silence. I sat up to peek through the puckered O of the wagon cover, and cursed softly.

Snow had begun to fall again, with such swiftness that the world was already freshly buried in it. Beauty muttered and stomped almost noiselessly in eight or ten inches, scowling at me when I scrambled out to brush its depth from the wagon seat and to begin harnessing her again.

"It may be better to wait it out, Amber."

"It would have been better if we'd stayed at the last village, or gone on to the next," I replied. Neither, though, had appealed to us; the villages were more isolated in this part of the country, or farther off the track, as Annalise's had been. Staying in the last one would have lost us half an afternoon's journey, and going to the next would have lost us half a night's sleep. "Beauty will probably be all right if it just keeps coming straight down like this, but the wind is likely to pick up, and she's too exposed. Either we go into the forest to try to build a rough shelter, or we hitch up and go on."

I looked back to see that, although he'd objected, Father was clearing more snow from the wagon bench before he pulled one of the straw-filled pillows from beneath the wagon's cover to sit on. Once I had her in the harness, I gave Beauty a nose bag and a scratch beneath the forelock. She gave me an impatient eye roll in return, but she put her head down, started munching oats, and plodded forward through the snow. I leapt onto the bench to sit beside Father and, wrapping my cloak around myself, peered toward the horizon.

We were hours from dawn: there was no hint of light anywhere, only the noiseless snow softening the edges of the world and weighing tree branches until they bowed and scraped our wagon's cover. Father, breath steaming in the cold, said, "You should climb inside, so when I'm frozen through you can drive."

"Imagine how awful this would be if you

were alone." I did as I'd been bade, nestling back into what warmth remained, and, to my surprise, I fell asleep to the sounds of wheels squeaking faintly as they packed snow, and of Beauty's steady footsteps.

I awakened hours later to a jolting stop and a curse. Alarmed, I pushed back out of the wagon to find Father with a lap full of snow and a disoriented expression. "Father?"

"I fell asleep." He stood, brushing snow off his lap, and shook himself. I climbed all the way out, standing beside him on the footboard, and looked around us in dismay.

Daylight had arrived in the form of dusky, snow-laden grey light that did hardly any more to light the way than full night had, but we were clearly no longer on the main road. We hadn't been for some time, it appeared: trees grew up around us almost close enough to touch, the path beneath us no more than a single track. The snow immediately surrounding us was no more than ankle deep, but five steps ahead of Beauty, it rose feathery-looking and chest deep. Beauty, undisturbed by this, took a few steps forward, then paused to look back at us, as if making sure we wanted her to go on.

The snow in front of her dropped to ankle depth for as many more steps as she'd taken, and remained banked tall and relentless beyond that. Father said, "Whoa," to her, weakly, and after a moment of gaping I scrambled through the wagon to look out the back pucker.

There was no sign of our passage what-so-ever. Five steps behind us, snow lay chest-deep again, as if it had lain undisturbed since winter began. I called, "Back her up a few steps, Father," as if there might be a way out of a thing I already knew in my bones. The wagon lurched and backed up, and, after five steps, pressed against the bank of snow. The snow gave a little, collapsing and sliding under the wagon's belly, but it most certainly did not disappear the way it was doing in *front* of Beauty. After another step or two backward, the snow impacted enough to stop the wagon's progress. Up front, Beauty nickered impatiently and eased forward again into unimpeded space.

I sat hard onto one of the benches, a sick flutter of missed heartbeats occupying my attention for a few unpleasant breaths. Then, cold with more than the weather, I made my way forward again to say, in a strange voice unlike my own, "We've been enchanted."

"Yes." Father sat on the bench again, heavily, and I sat beside him, the two of us staring wordlessly at the tall snow beyond us. There was nothing to be *done* about an enchantment, and no value in protesting that such things didn't really happen. No one properly believed they *did* happen, or at least, that they *still* happened, but sitting in a twenty foot rolling rectangle of shallow snow made it quite clear that they did still happen on occasion.

"We're going to have to go forward," I said after a while. "We might as well, before we get cold. The snow is still coming down."

Father shook first himself, then the reins, and Beauty, with a tail twitch that suggested it was about time, plodded forward. Enchantments, it seemed, did not distress enormous grumpy mares. Nor did I feel *distressed*, precisely. Stunned, perhaps, but— but, well, Pearl was a witch, and the Border Wars had been fought against faeries, and our country's queen was old beyond reason, and if those things could be, then a forest might be enchanted too, and we were lucky it hadn't gotten us before.

I sat up straighter. "Father, is this *our* forest?"

He gave me a look somewhere between amusement and the suspicion the snow had made me simple. "I suppose it is, but how do you tell the difference between the end of one forest and the beginning of another? If you mean, are we close to home, I have no idea. I don't know how long I slept, save for it still being dark when I'd last opened my eyes. It could be nine or noon, now, though, for all I know." He gestured at the indistinct sky's inability to hint at the hour. "I don't think we'll find our way home through the forest, if that's what you're asking."

"No. It's just that the villagers wouldn't hunt in our forest."

"Oh. *Oh.* The beast protecting it. An enchantment itself. I see." Father looked around more carefully, as if, now that he understood me, he might see a landmark to orient us with. I looked, too, and although we were neither of us talking as we searched, a different kind of silence came over us as we began to understand what we saw.

Beyond our peculiar little rectangle of safety, where the snow still fell constantly and swiftly, a ferocious storm raged. Had clearly *been* raging all along, but until we began to look hard, we had been as protected from knowledge of it as we were from its ravages. The more I watched, the more I realized that the trees just beyond us danced and rattled with wind, and the harder I listened, the more clearly I could hear that wind howling and shrieking, as if enraged it couldn't reach us. The snow outside of our enchantment didn't merely fall, but whipped and lashed and spun, creating a whiteout that we would never have been able to pass through safely.

I remembered Pearl's reading of the cards, and wondered, with a shudder, what would have happened if I had not been with Father. I said nothing, though, and rather than guess at our location, we rode on in silence, letting the enchantment guide us through the storm.

I looked up when Beauty stopped again as darkness fell, then stood, shaking snow off my blanket and quilt, to gape at iron gates twenty feet tall set into stone walls their equal in height. Father had gone back into the wagon to rest; I tried to say his name and produced only a squeak.

Beauty stood not two lengths from the gates, which, like our enchanted rectangle, were enveloped in a hard, steady snowfall nothing like the howling maelstrom surrounding them. I hadn't seen them before she stopped, either more magic or the storm itself blocking them until their enchantment melded with ours.

The gates were laden with a copper design that took every advantage of the metal's natural properties: golden-red roses 'grew' all over them, stems and leaves blueish-green with patina. The girl I had been a year ago admired the artistry, and the one I was now felt sorry for the servants who had to polish the roses while leaving the stems rough and green. Then again, the gates were clearly protected by charms, anyway, so perhaps the roses stayed polished of their own volition.

As if I'd guessed a secret and earned passage, the gates swung open—inward, silent, brushing snow into arches as they passed over it—to invite us down a long straight avenue lined with massive oak trees. The length of the road and the whiteness of oncoming night hid what lay at the road's end, but I remained on my feet, swaying with the wagon's motion, to await what would be revealed.

Even expecting it, it made me laugh. A manor house — a *palace* — with wings unfolding from a central edifice, rounded facades that spoke of ballrooms, ground level arched doors in the straighter sections, no doubt leading to storage, stables, kitchens; towers at corners, wide shallow — and currently frozen, but cleared to skate on — ponds carefully kept in beautifully sculpted basins; gardens that backed onto forest, and all of it unheard of, a hidden castle in the woods. The gates could lead to nothing else; the enchantment that had saved us could hardly lead to anything else, and I laughed again at the astonishing absurdity of it.

Father, hearing my laugh, opened the front of the wagon cover, and breathed, "Sweet mother of the stars," in genuine reverence.

Beauty ambled around the ponds, stopping, as if a stablehand came to stand at her head, directly in front of the sweeping stairs that climbed to the castle's main doors. Father and I sat there like lumps, and after a minute or so, the doors — themselves easily ten feet in height, and carved with the same rose relief as the gates — opened.

"You go," Father finally said. "I'll…bring Beauty to the stables."

"You want me to go into an enchanted castle *alone*?"

"Ah," Father said. "Well. When you put it that way —"

Beauty stomped a foot impatiently, drawing our attention to her. The reins slipped, causing me to lurch for them, but a pecularity in *how* they slipped made me look again, and then swallow. "Father, is someone…holding…that rein?"

It looked for all the world like someone was: a firm but fair hand, like Flint's, just below Beauty's dribbling chin. As we watched, the rein tugged a little, not quite enough to coax Beauty into action, but more than enough to jolt Father and myself out of the wagon to see what was going on.

No sooner than we were on the ground than the reins' tension increased, and Beauty walked placidly away in the wake of an invisible guide, leaving us alone in the snow with an inviting door already opened to us.

"It's an impossible castle in an enchanted snowstorm in a haunted forest," I said in a voice slightly more shrill than I had hoped for. "Naturally there are invisible servants to care for the horses."

"Naturally." Father sounded as rattled as I, which made me feel a little better. Together we mounted the stairs, I, at least, having already given up on an expectation of a footman or butler standing at the door to greet us.

Nor was I disappointed: the door had, by all appearances, opened on its own, just as it then gracefully closed behind us. I caught a glimpse, as it closed, of the storm closing in: the magnitude of the enchantment, it seemed, had been for our benefit, and not simply the magical manner of the place keeping its personal weather mild for the season. I tugged my cloak around me, aware, as I had not been before, that it was wet and cold, and turned to examine our shelter.

A foyer of preposterous size stretched before us, with a golden carpet nine feet wide laid over a parquet floor that glowed from the reflected light of beeswax candles lining the foyer walls. Massive curved stairways to our left and right led to ornately-railed halls on the floor above. Beneath the overhanging hallway, the foyer darkened ominously, and I shrieked when a pair of gentle hands settled on my shoulders as if to remove my cloak.

The hands, startled, disappeared at my shriek. Father and I both spun around to find no one there at all. I clutched my heart and my cloak, wild-eyed with something between laughter and fear. "Invisible servants," I said again, once more shrilly, and swept my cloak off before I could reconsider the action. There was hardly a moment's hesitation before the cloak's weight left my hands, and then, as if to entice us, the pop and crackle off a hearth fire suddenly lit the distant darkness of the foyer. Father handed his wet cloak to the invisible servant as well, and we went, with great haste, toward the fire.

By the time we arrived at it there were dry clothes waiting for us, and a changing shield with its warm side to the fire, that we might dress in privacy without sacrificing any moment of warmth. I hadn't realized how cold I was until we were out of it, nor how damp with snow all my clothes had become. I pulled on soft, thick stockings and whimpered at the warmth and comfort of them, and gratefully layered myself in petticoats, a dress, and shawls before emerging from behind the changing shield.

Fur slippers awaited me, and a hat and muff. I pulled them on and sat on a thick fur in front of the fire, shivering because I was now warming up. Moments later Father, as bundled and comfortable-looking as I felt, joined me. We hugged, as much to reassure each other of *our* normality, at least, and fell back with sheepish smiles. A scrape sounded behind us and I turned to find two large, comfortable chairs had appeared, and between them, a small wooden table with two enormous, steaming mugs resting on it. "Oh, stars. Is that cider?"

It was, and no other drink in all my life warmed me so much as that mug did that day.

Its rich, sweet, spicy flavor needed no alcohol to bring on weariness: the long day's travel through the snow, and the tremendous warmth of the fire, did that job. I drank the cider faster, determined to have it finished before sleep took me, and later, could only suppose that I'd succeeded, as I awoke eventually nestled in the same chair, and without cider spilled on my clothes.

Father had stretched out on the fur in front of the fire and was snoring gently. I chortled and went in search of a necessary, which I would never have found if an exquisitely detailed panel in the wall had not happened to open and reveal a latrine with a chamber pot. I said, "Thank you," to the empty air, and went about my business, wondering if invisible servants had senses of smell and whether it was unpleasant for them to empty latrines.

The necessary dealt with, I crept to the tall windows by the front doors and peered outside, where the only alleviation from the pitch-black night was the snow swirling madly around the palace. I could hardly hear it, even at the window, and so returned to the fire, grateful to sleep the rest of the night and wait out the storm.

In my absence, someone had brought a chaise in and placed it as close to the fire as it would fit without resting on Father. I whispered, "Thank you!" again, and crawled on to it, asleep within moments.

The scent of breakfast woke me again some time later. Eggs, toasted bread, bacon—oh, stars, *bacon!*—crisply-flavored apple juice, scones with salted butter and jelly: Father woke to the sounds of my feasting, and we both ate until our bellies ached. "All right," I said when I could eat no more, "I admit there's something to be said for unadulterated luxury."

"I could marry even Pearl off, with this bacon as her dowry," Father said with a smile, then lifted his gaze to the room and added, somewhat awkwardly, "Thank you."

An agreeable silence responded, and we sighed as one with content. "The storm hadn't stopped yet, last night, but I wonder if we can find our way to Beauty. I'm sure she's fine, but I'd like to check on her."

A handful of candles lit immediately, and then, when we didn't rise, a few more beyond them came to life as well. Father and I exchanged glances, ending with me shrugging my eyebrows and stealing another scone. "Lead on," I said to the candles, and, nibbling on the scone, followed the castle's guidance through tall, echoing halls down to a modest door that led into the stables.

Beauty stood fat and glossy in a stall, so full of hay and grain that she leaned lazily against one of the box walls with her eyelids drooping sleepily. She'd been brushed to a shine, and her feathery leg hair was fluffed and lovely. I got her an apple she absolutely didn't need, and she slobbered it from my hand more graciously than usual. Then I pushed the stable door open, finding the estate outside a glittering wonderland under icy clear blue skies. Father came to stand with me at the door a moment before letting out a long, relieved breath. "I'll harness Beauty, and we can begin to find our way home."

"What, and offend our invisible hosts?" I asked, amused. "Wait five minutes, then turn around, and I bet you'll find her harnessed and ready to go. I wonder if the road is clear, though." Not that there'd *been* a road, or not one worth mentioning. Just the rolling patch of shallow snow attending us so we could make our way to the hidden palace in the woods. "Or if the enchantment will clear a path...."

"The enchantment brought us this far. We may as well trust it to the end." An odd note came into Father's voice. I looked askance at him, but he shook his head, passing it off, so I let it pass as well.

"Five minutes," I wagered. "I'm going to take that five minutes to look around a little. I might skate across those ponds."

"In your boots?"

"I wouldn't be surprised if there are skates waiting for me," I said blithely, and went forth into the blinding morning.

It was quiet until I picked the rose.

There were, in fact, skates waiting for me at the pond. I fastened them to my shoes and flew across ice that had been blown or swept clear since the storm's end, spinning clumsily and laughing. The ponds took me all the way to the palace's other wing, using considerably more than five minutes I'd promised Father, but rather than turn back, I removed the skates and marched onward through the snow, eager to see the gardens that lined the estate's perimeter. Even now, in the dead of winter, they were lushly green, that darkest green of winter blooms, and splashes of red and white stood out against them, like holly berries and snow in clumps the size of my hand. I waded through shallow snow—regardless of the storm's ferocity, it appeared the palace allowed only a few inches of accumulation—until I'd reached the climbing bushes, but long before that, I knew it wasn't holly at all, but roses.

The blooms came in every color from snowiest white to the deepest crimson red, and they *were* the size of my hand. They grew together indiscriminately, no apparent care for whether blooms of different colors should appear on the same bush; some, in a nod to their unusual situation, blushed red to white, or white to red, while others ran a gamut of pinks with their hearts or their outer petals curling to blood tones. Their scent was enriching, delicious enough to drink and so heavy I felt I could climb the sweet smell all the way to the sky.

If I could make perfume of *these*, we might wend our way back into wealth after all. A cutting *might* survive, if I kept it close to my heart on the drive home, and tended it carefully in a warm spot for the winter. Without any particular thought of wrongdoing, I chose an especially gorgeous, sturdy-looking bloom, and plucked it from the bush.

A roar of crippling weight broke the morning's quiet and drove me to the ground. I knotted my hands over my head, the rose tangling in my hair, and screamed as if my smaller cry could break the power of the large one. Wind howled around me, smashing petals and leaves to the snowy ground and breaking branches over my back, so wicked thorns snagged in my borrowed clothes. Shards of snow and ice drove into my hands where they covered my head, and I clenched my eyes tight against the turmoil, whispering a prayer to the sun and her sister moon that I might be saved from the storm.

Whether it was the power of my prayer or — more likely — that a little time accustomed me to the dreadful weight of the roaring, I began to hear words in the wind, distorted by powerful rage, but words none-the-less: *How dare you take my rose*, the wind demanded. *Is it*

not enough I have warmed you, fed you, clothed
you? Is it not enough to have saved you from the
storm? Are you so ungrateful a wretch as to
require the very heart of my garden as well?

No: it was not prayer, or even time that
accustomed me to the terrible sound. It was
that the sound *approached* me, clarifying as it
came closer. Little by little I unwound from the
earth, eyes still fastened on the ground, until I
sat on my heels with the offending rose
piercing tiny, agonizing holes in my palms. As
the roaring came to an end, I closed my fingers
around the thorny stem, as if the pain would
lend me strength, and with that borrowed
strength, I lifted my gaze to look upon a Beast.

From my vantage, kneeling on the ground,
the Beast looked some eight feet tall, and half
again that wide at its terrible shoulders. It fell
forward onto all fours, thrusting a huge,
massive face with fetid breath at mine, and I
was, of all things, reminded of little Jet, trying
to get Maman's attention, and putting his face
so close to hers that her eyes would cross and
she couldn't properly see him at all.

Undone by a combination of that thought
and terror, I laughed.

The Beast reared back, confusion and
offense obvious even on an utterly inhuman
face. I could see it more clearly from the little
distance, and whatever laughter I had died in

my throat, but for that moment I had taken, if not an upper hand, at least an equal one, and the Beast did not know how to respond.

Neither, in fairness, did I. Its face was a mockery of a man's, as though its maker had begun with that template but had no idea of what features were meant to rest on a human form. Heavy brows, like a ram's, furrowed over small, boar-like eyes, and short, thick twisting horns swept back from its brow, giving its head too much length and the look of something that could batter down a door, or face a bull. Its face was flatter than a boar or ram's, with highly rounded cheekbones framing a muzzle that could have been a lion's compressed to the depth of a man's profile. A hare lip gave way to an overbiting lower jaw, from whence tusks as long as my finger protruded, and I wondered that it didn't cut its own face with the motion of its jaw. A tangled mane of fur flew back from its face and jowls and ran freely over its shoulders, only becoming shorter along hugely muscled arms. Brutal-looking clawed hands dug into the earth not three steps away from me, and made it clear that I could be as easily rent as the soil.

I concluded in that moment that I preferred to die on my feet, and lurched to them, still clinging to the rose. With the Beast on all fours, and me on my feet, I was the taller of us, though its shoulders were nearly at the level of my eyes, and its mane bristled some distance down its spine, lending it more height. Its neck, though, was not suited to looking up from a position of all fours, and so in order to see me, it backed up several steps. Although I knew better, the effect was of its retreat, and my confidence regained a little ground again.

At least, it did until the Beast shook itself, growling, and rose to a human stance again, teaching me that it *was* near enough to eight feet tall. Its torso was as misshapen as its face, a deep bullish chest whittling to a waist strangely narrow by comparison; beasts were not meant to stand as men, and to do so threw its dimensions off in a way my mind could not entirely accept. Its haunches and knees and ankles were lion-like, bent all around the wrong way for a man, and massive clawed back feet suggested it could leap across half the estate in a single effort.

It was wearing trousers.

Everything else, its mismade form, its violence, its earth-shattering roar, came to a stop in the face of that unexpected discovery. Beasts—animals of the forest and jungles, or even the farmlands—did not wear clothing. Whatever this Beast was, he—and it was, I felt certain, a *he*, as it lacked any kind of breasts and a female Beast would, in my estimation, wear a dress to cover herself in the same way this male one retained his modesty—he was not an unthinking monster. A monster, yes, but not a mindless one.

Nor could he be, if he had been roaring words at me, so I might have realized sooner that he was not entirely an animal. On the other hand, my heart had not yet calmed and I still swayed with fear, so it had not, perhaps, been very long since his tumultuous arrival. Before I could speak, another of his bellows split the air: "*How dare you take my rose?*"

I took a step back, more from the force of his shout than fear; somehow the trousers had restored my equilibrium to an astonishing degree. My voice, however, was more tremulous than I preferred when I replied. "How could I possibly know I wasn't meant to?"

He continued to roar as if he hadn't heard me, but I hadn't expected him to. I continued anyway, my voice still shaking, determination pushing it forward, if not volume. "I suppose I might have realized that everything had been *given*, without us asking for it. I suppose I might have realized that to *take*, under those circumstances, was ill-mannered. But I didn't. I'm sorry. You saved our lives, and I've repaid you badly. I hope you can forgive me."

"How much?" His tenor changed so quickly, the mighty voice dropping from a roar to a rumble so smoothly, that I almost didn't recognize the words as ones I knew. Even when I did, the meaning escaped me, and I made a small, confused gesture with the rose. "How much do you hope I can forgive you?"

he clarified.

I stared up—and up, and up—at him, and wondered what he expected as an answer. Wondered what I dared *give* him as an answer, and wondered whether it mattered at all. "I wouldn't die for it."

"Would you stay?"

Perhaps it was that a voice came from the Beast at all: maybe that was what made understanding the meaning of his words so difficult. "Stay? Stay *here*? With *you*?"

The Beast made a motion of surprising grace, encompassing the gardens, the palace, and himself. "Yes."

"I would rather not!"

"And what would you exchange instead? Your father? Your family? The village, which feasts uninvited on the beasts of my forest?"

"Exch—the vill—do you mean to say an *object* must remain here in exchange for the rose, in order to earn your forgiveness? And what do you mean, your forest? The lodge is ours, and the forest ours to hunt! And you can't take an entire village in exchange for a *rose*, that's preposterous. What would you do with it?" I looked around the garden, imagining the enormous grounds beyond them, and reconsidered. "The villagers' lives would probably be much easier here, with the obliging snowfall and the invisible servants. Not that I intend to *trade* them for your *rose*, but—"

"Someone must pay. The roses are precious to me. If you refuse to stay, I will take something else in exchange. You have sisters, brothers. Perhaps one of them."

"Over my dead body!"

"That," the Beast snarled, suddenly very large and angry again, "can be arranged."

I cringed, cutting my hands on the rose's thorns again, and that was how my father found us: me quailing before a looming Beast. He threw himself between us, all his age forgotten in the defense of his child, and I saw with a shock that he carried a sword, a weapon I didn't believe he'd touched since his days in the Border Wars. The Beast raised an enormous paw to slap him away, and Father darted to one side, piercing the monster's hand with his blade. The Beast roared so deeply that snow fell from the rosebushes. He closed his hand around the sword, yanking away from Father, and withdrew it from his own paw to hold in his uninjured hand. It looked diminished in his grasp, like a trifle or a toy, but he wielded it with strange competency, reversing the blade as if he would bring it down to impale my father.

I flung myself in front of Father, screaming, "No!", and the Beast growled, "Someone must pay."

"A rose isn't worth a *life!*"

The Beast lifted his bloody paw-like hand, roaring, "This is more than a rose!"

I pushed Father back and advanced furiously on the Beast. "He was protecting me, which he wouldn't have needed to do if you weren't being so terrifying over a stupid rose! You'll heal! The rosebush isn't harmed for having lost one bloom! But you will *not* slay my father over a rose, or steal away any of my family, or the villagers, or anyone else! I picked the rose! If you're so determined that someone has to stay to pay for it, then yes, I'll stay! And I'll make you regret it until your dying day!"

Father blurted, "Amber," in horror, and the Beast began to laugh, a deep, bitter sound that reverberated off the frozen ground and distant estate walls. "If you can bring about my dying day, I will welcome your presence here more profoundly than you will ever know. Go," he said more sharply to Father. "Be grateful that your daughter is as bold as she is lovely." He turned on a massive paw and clumped away through the garden, leaving us alone.

I hadn't realized, until he left, that the Beast's presence made the air feel heavier, like a storm was coming. No wonder: I'd hardly had time to. My shoulders slumped and I curled my hand around—around the rose, thorns prickling my palm again. I'd forgotten I even still held the cursed thing, and I began to cast it away, then thought again. If it was going to cause so much trouble, then at the very least I would keep it. Not for cuttings to make perfume from, not if I was to remain here—or maybe I *would* grow it, and make perfume anyway, just to be spiteful—but if not that, to press and dry, and that, too, would be for spite. So instead of throwing it away, I put it down in the snow carefully, where I could collect it later, and looked at the dots of blood rising from my palm.

They sparkled faintly, as if this place made something so mundane as bleeding a magical process, too. Wonderful: that would make my moon bloods a splendid experience, here. I sighed, curled my hand around the thorn-pricks, and turned to face my father, who had been ranting since the Beast's departure, and to whom I had not been listening. I didn't need to. I knew he would be speaking of the Beast's horrors and forbidding me to stay while also demanding to know how it was I had come to promise to stay, and, indeed, such was the content of his speech. When he finally fell silent, awaiting my explanations, I only said, "You should take Beauty and leave now, Father, before any more of the day is lost."

He said, "No," with such finality that I didn't bother arguing. I had very little doubt that one way or another, the Beast would see him on his way very soon, and I was grateful for a few more hours of human company. "What happened, Amber?"

"I picked a rose. Our host objected." My mild response amused me, and I began to laugh. Not a healthy, full laugh; that I knew. It was fed by fear and absurdity and the tingling pain in my hand, but it was laughter, and I was grateful for that, too. When it ran its course, I added, "He *is* the Beast of our forest, and threatened the villagers for feasting on the forest's beasts, if I didn't stay. Or the family. He threatened them too. So I'm staying."

"I'll stay!"

"You didn't pick the rose."

"I'm old, Amber. My life is near enough to over already. What does it matter if a Beast kills me?"

"It matters very much to me!" I glanced behind me at the Beast's dreadful footprints. "Besides, I don't think he's going to kill me. He had ample opportunity while I was cowering and screaming, and he seemed quite specific about *taking* villagers, or someone from the family, not killing them."

"So you intend to remain his prisoner here forever?"

I looked toward the palace and said, "There are worse prisons," hollowly. "Perhaps he'll let me go sometime. After the lifespan of a rose."

Father's voice dropped. "These roses are blooming in the dead of winter, Amber. How long do you think their lifespan is?"

I crouched to collect the flower that had

started all the trouble, and gestured with it as I stood. "Well, I should be able to make some astonishing perfumes with it, if it lasts forever."

"*Amber!*"

"I'd better find some humor in it, Father, gallows or otherwise, or I'll go mad before you've even left the gates." I offered him a brief, determined smile. "Now let's go back to the castle so I can write a goodbye letter to the family for you to bring home."

I heard the shape of my name on his inhalation, the protestation he wanted to make, but somehow he held it back, for which I was grateful. Instead he offered me his arm. I tucked mine through it, and we walked in silence back to the palace that was now my prison.

The letter ought to have been difficult to write. Instead it came smoothly from my pen, a recitation of facts so peculiar that there seemed no profit in trying to explain them: either they would be accepted, or they would not. Father would back my story up, and Pearl, I knew, would believe me. I wondered again what might have happened if I had not gone with Father. A death, Pearl had said. Maybe none of this would even have transpired; perhaps something would have gone wrong in the city.

I didn't believe that, though. I thought he would have died in the storm, or perhaps worst of all, been rescued by the enchantment only to pick the wretched rose himself, as a gift for me, because he knew I liked them. I thought he would have died here, at the Beast's hands, for that transgression, and just imagining that version of events was worse than staying here myself.

Father and I walked down to the stables again together when I'd finished the letter. Beauty stood ready in her harness, already hitched to the wagon, but the wagon sat lower than it had when we'd arrived. I glanced through the tightly-drawn cover and let out a sharp laugh. "Father."

He paused in climbing to the driver's seat and looked into the wagon. "Mother of stars."

For a little while we were both occupied in going through the wagon's contents, which were as generous—more generous—than the meals and clothes we'd been given since our arrival. There were books, stacks of them that beggared the few we'd bought in the city to replace those we'd lost in the fire. Prominent among the gift books was a copy of one we had been unable to find in the city: a compilation of geological and mythological information about the earth and stones. We children had all been named for rocks inside its pages, and *as* children, we girls had loved poring over the beautifully inked drawings that represented our namesakes. That small volume's loss had been one of the things we could hardly bear to think about, and our inability to find another copy had been quietly heartbreaking. To see it here amongst the Beast's gifts broke my heart again, in another way.

Beneath the books, well. *Most* of the fabric was practical: tightly woven linens and wools in varying weights, and mostly colors that would either dye well or wear well, showing little dirt. A little of it, though, was raw silk, for a few really fine dresses. *Most* of the coins were spendable: bits of nickel or copper, silver pennies and ingots of iron that could be spent or shaped. Some were gold, though, and only of any use to us in the city.

There was nothing practical about any of the jewels, but then, jewels were never meant for practical purposes. Some were small enough for trade, but one chest, when opened, revealed seven polished stones settled in a circle against black velvet. A rectangle of jet could only be seen against the velvet because of its shine; a round-cornered triangle of brick-red jasper threaded with white quartz looked shockingly decadent in comparison. A thick arrowhead of waxy pink flint, lined in white, completed the top half of the circle. Below them lay an opal the size and shape of a partridge's egg, a square of dark grey granite flecked with blue, and an heart-shaped garnet as large as my thumbnail.

In the midst of them, though, placed in the middle of the other six, lay a perfect tear-drop pearl four inches long. I couldn't bring myself to even touch it, my fingers hovering above the jewel. I was no witch, but I could feel the pearl's energy pressing toward my fingertips. Spreading my hands over the whole chest made both hands tingle, as if every stone in the box was laden with enchantment.

I couldn't tell if Father was angry or afraid— perhaps both—when he said, "This Beast seems to know us very well. That pearl, though. Why such a treasure?"

I heard myself say, "Because Pearl is a witch," somewhat distantly as I gently closed the chest. Father flinched when I did, as if he'd been enchanted *by* the jewels, but then he heard what I'd said and shook off the enchantment for surprise.

"She is?"

"I think so. You'll have to ask her. But if she is, she'll be able to focus great magic through that pearl. He does know us very well. I suppose he would, if we've been living in his forest." I was obscurely, and absurdly, hurt that there had been no jewel for me. I'd cast my lot in with the Beast, but to have him divorce me from my family so thoroughly, so swiftly, made my heart ache with a too-fast beat. "Wait. Before you go, Father." I ran back into the palace to the parlor we'd been housed in, and collected the wretched rose that had started my troubles. I brought it back to him, tucking it into his coat. "If I'm going to be condemned for picking it, then the least it can do is start a new rose garden in my name. I think Flint will have the knack of caring for it."

"Amber," Father said in dismay. "I want nothing of the Beast's roses. Or any of the rest of this. I only want you to come home with me."

"We are not to get what we want, though, Father." I took a deep breath. "You had better go. If you don't go now I don't know if I can bear it."

"Then I won't go," he said ferociously, but somehow, within minutes, we had embraced and I stood alone at the head of the long driveway, watching the wagon grow smaller with distance.

"He'll be home before dark," the Beast rumbled from behind me, and I, with all the grace and poise of a startled child, shrieked and jolted away from him. When I turned, he stood a few feet away, a huge dark blot against the snow, but with evident surprise written across his horrible face. "I didn't mean to startle you. I thought you would like to know he would make it home safely and quickly, within an hour or two."

I did want to know that. I also did not at all want to be in any way grateful to the Beast. I stared at him with the anger of having been frightened and the fear of what came next, and the abrupt, overwhelming loneliness of abandonment, even if I'd accepted the path myself. Very suddenly I was on the verge of tears, which was worse than anything else.

The Beast stared back at me, and, apparently recognizing the disaster about to erupt, said, "Let me show you to your rooms." He turned swiftly, dropping to all fours as he did so, and paced away.

He had a tail. I hadn't noticed when he'd left the garden earlies, but he had a tail. A bear's tail, short and waggily and not at all in keeping with the general size and ferocity of him. Except it was, because bears, after all, were large and ferocious. But they were also round through the waist and hip, whereas the Beast narrowed more like a lion. I might have expected a longer, lashing tail, but not the stubbly little thing that stuck out from the back of his trousers.

I wiped the back of my hand across my eyes, and followed the Beast and his ridiculous little tail back to the palace.

The palace doors swept open ahead of us, and closed again behind us with the dignity of enchantment. I remembered with a pang how I hadn't even seen Glover in the room as Father and I discussed what to do, the night we fled the city. Servants were already invisible to their masters; what real difference did it make if they were in *fact* invisible? "Are they real?"

The Beast understood my question, which was intriguing and uncomfortable all at once. "As real as you or I."

Given that he was an eight foot tall Beast in an enchanted castle, and I was the sister of a witch, I thought it wiser not to consider that definition of reality any farther. The Beast led me up the right side of the sweeping stairway, and only a small distance down the corridor before pausing at a door, and opening it. "Your rooms."

Considering what little I'd seen of the rest of the palace, I expected the space I entered to be sumptuous. Nor was I disappointed: the door opened on a sitting room with a fire already crackling in its hearth. Woven rugs lay beneath animal furs to keep the floor's chill well away from the feet, and there were all the accoutrements one might expect in a civilized sitting space: liquor sideboards, tables, comfortable chairs, all done in rosewoods and golden fabrics. Beyond that, through another doorway, I caught a glimpse of the bedroom, replete with a canopied bed and windows that let sunlight spill generously across the floor. All well and good; I would look to it in a moment. But something in the sitting room had caught my eye. I crossed to a six-shelf bookcase filled to overflowing, and said, under my breath, "Maybe this won't be so bad."

"You like to read," the Beast said as I took a familiar title down. I nodded, turning through the pages, and he said, "There is a library."

I turned, surprised, the book still in hand. "You mean, more than this?"

"Considerably more."

I put the book down. "Can I see?"

The Beast gave me a look that, had it come from Pearl, I would have called pedantic, and I muttered, "*May* I see," rather than wait to discover I had traded a beautiful literalist of a sister for a dreadful literalist of a Beast.

A sound emanated from his chest, and after a moment I judged it a chuckle. I felt my mouth pinch into sourness, and the Beast's chuckle became a laugh that reverberated in my bones. "This way," he said, and I followed him in a dudgeon warped with rueful amusement. He was a monster keeping me against my will, but, his initial rage at my picking the rose having passed, he seemed a rather reasonable captor. I was not, at the moment, either afraid or resentful: the prospect of a library and an enchanted castle were intriguing enough to allow me to pretend that this was nothing more than a temporary adventure to be embraced. The reality would settle in soon enough.

We went up another set of stairs, back across the corridor above the foyer, and a little more deeply into the hall than my room had been. The Beast opened a door on the opposite side of the hall from mine, and I stepped onto a balcony overlooking three open floors in one of the round-fronted rooms facing the front gardens.

Bookshelves and reading nooks lined the walls of each floor, heavily carpeted balconies, like the one I stood on, growing larger as they approached the distant ground floor. I glanced up at a glass domed roof, and smiled at the effect: from here, the architecture made it seem as though we were nestled in an enormous egg, its shell made of books. I drew my hand along the satin-smooth balcony rail as I walked around it, a foolish smile on my face. Almost halfway around, part of the floor dropped into a bannistered stairway that led down to the next level. I followed it down, and then the next one down again, making half-circles of the library until I reached the ground floor and walked to its middle to look up at the egg-shaped balconies. The Beast paced a little way behind me on all fours, not rising to his — hind feet, I supposed — until we reached the bottom floor. "The top balcony, just below the dome, is an iris. It can be closed, and the dome becomes an ideal spot for star-gazing."

"Doesn't your breath steam it up?"

The Beast chuckled again, that deep sound more like a growl. "I suppose it should, but no."

Magic, I thought, but didn't say. I did say, "I

didn't know there were so many books in all the world."

"You are educated." That was a question, though he didn't phrase it as one. I dropped my chin in a scant nod, still gazing upward, and the Beast went on, "You know, perhaps, that over the centuries, much knowledge has been lost. Libraries have been deliberately burned or otherwise sacked."

My lip curled. "Yes."

"This library seems to have...saved...those books. Copied them, or stolen them before ruin took them, or...something of that nature. I've found books here that are referenced by *other* books, more modern books, as lost to time. I think it's possible that every piece of deliberately preserved writing is stored here, somewhere."

I turned to him, astonished. "Scholars from all over the world would die to come here."

"As it turns out," the Beast said, "people prefer to kill than to die for something, and I am a Beast."

I stood with that a moment, absorbing it and all of its implications, before turning away. The Beast stepped back. "If you're hungry, ask the servants. Otherwise, if you care to join me for dinner, they'll let you know when it's ready, and bring you to the dining hall."

He left, and I had to watch from the corner of my eye so I could judge the moment, just as he crossed the threshold, to call, "Do I have a choice?"

He hesitated, a massive paw on the door and his head turned a little toward me, although he made no effort to meet my eye. "You always have a choice."

I neither read nor ate, but spent a few hours wandering the library. Books tended to return to the shelves after lying fallow a few minutes, if I'd taken them down to examine. After several iterations of that, I cleared my throat. "You don't have to do that, you know. I'll clean up after myself. I mean, if you want to, go ahead, but don't feel obliged."

I felt a hum in the air, as if an urgent discussion took place just out of earshot. Then the most recent book I'd taken down rose from the table I'd put it on, and settled itself firmly back into place on the shelves. I laughed. "All right. Thank you."

The air hummed again, and I went about my business a while longer before climbing into the dome through a staircase built neatly into the shelves. Gold-painted lead joined the windows, each of which were a tremendous arching triangle of glass that ran from floor to roof. They warped a little near the bottoms, showing their age, but the clarity at eye-height and above astonished me.

The Beast's palace was a patch of tamed

land in the midst of a forest that went on forever on all sides. I had no sense which direction home lay; there were no tell-tale threads of smoke rising to indicate our village, or any other, nor any cut in the forest roof to suggest a river running through it. The treetops were black and white with winter right now, but in the summer I imagined the green leaves would look like a carpet that could be walked on all the way to the edge of the world.

It was hard to tell where exactly the rose gardens ended and the forest began, even with the high stone wall that surrounded the palace grounds. At the front of the palace, along the driveway, the demarcation was clear enough, but forest and roses grew together beyond that, as if the forest intended to one day encroach upon, and defeat, the palace at its heart.

I shivered, deciding the dome was perhaps best left for night, when all that could be seen were the stars. It only took a few minutes to work my way back to my room, the long halls offering scant temptation to explore them. There would be plenty of time to do that, and I was both hungry and tired.

A fire still crackled in my room, and the book I'd taken down now sat on a table beside a chair before the fire. I brushed my fingers over it on the way by, saying, "Thank you," again, but went to investigate the bedroom I hadn't looked at earlier.

Sunset was coming on, and in its light, my room swam like a pool of gold. The bed's clothes were a dark sky blue, embroidered with fanciful beasts and birds of gold, and its frame, like the rest of the furniture in the room, was of golden oak, rich but not dark with age. The furniture covers were done in blue and gold as well, though a deeper shade of blue, and the floor, where it could be seen beneath rugs and furs, glowed as golden as the furniture. The walls were tapestry-lined, keeping warmth in, but they too were light in shade, and picked with threads of gold. It was not just the effect of the tidy hearth in one wall that made the room seem warmer than the rest of the palace, but the light and color. The Beast wanted me to like it here, which was either reassuring or disturbing, depending on how I wanted to think about it.

For the moment, I would take reassuring. I went to the vanity, which held as fine a mirror as I'd ever seen, and touched its table-top before laughing.

The mirror's frame and the table's edging were both amber, glowing pieces of polished gold that looked lovely against the table's blue and white streaked agate surface. A hand mirror entirely backed in amber lay on the table, and upon inspection, the comb in one drawer, and the brush beside it, were respectively of, and backed by, amber.

"Enough," I said, as if the servants could respond. "Perhaps too much, in fact. Thank you for welcoming me, but enough."

That almost-audible hum rustled the air again. I turned as if I could see the speakers, and instead found a gown lying on the bed. It was not amber-colored, and I wondered if that had been the topic my invisible servants were discussing; I wouldn't put it past them to have somehow changed the color while I was turning around. No, instead it was blue with lighter blue roses embroidered onto it—I hadn't been wearing blue when I arrived, and I wondered how they knew I liked it—had an underskirt of a dark, handsome red, and sleeves that hadn't lost their minds with frills and scoops. I had worn much more dramatic gowns when we lived in the city, but this one seemed suitable for dinner with a Beast, especially since I could put it on by myself.

By the time I went to inspect myself in the vanity mirror, one more thing had changed: a half-moon amber necklace lay on the blue agate, the pendant set in gold wire that bound it to a delicate chain. Crescent moon amber earrings lay beside it, but it was the necklace that knocked my breath away. I sank to the vanity's stool, collecting the pendant in my palm, and whispered, "So you hadn't forgotten me, after all."

I bowed my head and cried over the necklace a long time; long enough that when I had finally wept myself dry, I supposed dinner had been taken hours earlier, and that the Beast had presumed himself stood up. But I was fiercely hungry by then, so I rose and went in search of the dining hall, or at least the kitchen, and perhaps also the Beast.

None of those three things were difficult to find: I followed my nose — or maybe the subtle guidance of an invisible servant — to the dining room, beyond which presumably lay the kitchen, but I had no need to go that far: the Beast awaited me at a table that looked untouched. Or, rather, the Beast awaited me by the fire, near a table of food that looked untouched. I stopped in the doorway, fingers folded around the necklace. I'd wanted to wear it, to remind me of my family. Too late I wondered what wearing it might say to *him*.

He turned his head as he'd done when exiting the library: acknowledging me, but not looking at me. "Are you all right?"

There were far too many answers to that, available in a range of tones from tragic to sarcastic. I settled, after a long moment's silence, on, "Not particularly."

The Beast nodded as though he'd expected nothing less. He was better dressed than he had been earlier: not just trousers, but a well-tailored coat that did nothing to hide his bulk but hid a great deal of fur, and a cravat tied so neatly I assumed his invisible servants had done the job. "Don't you get awfully warm in that?"

He met my eyes, startled, and laughed. It appeared I had a capacity for surprising my host, which, given his claws and teeth, seemed like it could end badly for me. He didn't leap to rend me, though, only made a gesture at himself, at the clothes, and said, "Yes."

"But you wear it anyway."

"Particularly at mealtimes," he confessed. "It helps keep fur out of the food."

I didn't want to smile, but I did anyway. "Well, if you've gone to all that trouble, and there's all this food waiting, maybe we should eat. I'm starving. Not," I said a moment later, as we sat down, "*this* starving…"

The table was long enough to comfortably seat my entire family and the Beast besides, and laden from one end to another with food. Roast pheasant, half a boar, a rack of lamb despite the improbable season for such; sauces ranging from mint to cranberry and innumerable in between; vegetables with crispy brown edges from roasting in goose fat, and half a dozen bottles of wine. That was just what I could easily see. I had no doubt there were more delectables hidden away.

"I eat a great deal," the Beast said carefully.

My appetite momentarily drained away. "Is that why I'm here?"

"To be *eaten*?" The Beast sounded genuinely horrified. "No!"

I let out a shaky breath. "I supposed not, or you'd have slain me in the gardens and hung me for dinner. Unless you were planning to fatten me up first, in which case…" I took a bite of pheasant and slid down as far into the chair as my dress would let me, groaning with delight. "In which case it may be worth it. That bacon this morning was stupendous, too."

"I'm glad." The Beast had not quite recovered, it seemed, from my presumption that I was there as a meal. He watched me eat, and after a while, when I had stuffed myself nearly silly, I realized that he had *only* watched me eat, and not eaten anything himself.

"I thought you said you ate a lot."

"I do. Not, however, in company."

I considered the Beast's strange muzzle, his thrusting jaw and the deadly tusks that framed his face, and thought of wolves and cats eating. That in itself was a tearing, violent action, but their lower jaws were at least wired for it, not overbiting the upper jaw to an ungainly degree. "I assume it's an unsightly process."

The Beast nodded, and so did I. "Does that mean you've been waiting here hungry all evening, afraid to eat because I might show up unexpectedly and interrupt?"

"Something like that."

I put my napkin aside. "Then I should go, so you can eat in peace."

He tilted his vast head. "Why would you be kind enough to care?"

"I don't know." I waited on myself, seeing if any other answer surfaced, but none did, so I said again, "I don't know," and rose. "Good night, Beast."

His enormous chuckle rolled through the room. "'Beast'?"

Heat shot through me. "I'm sorry. I didn't even think to ask if you had a name."

"'Beast' will do. It is what I am, after all." He chuckled again, and I fled toward the door, arrested there by the sound of my name and a question: "Amber, will you sleep with me?"

"*Excuse* me?" I looked back, too astonished to be insulted, and thinking, impossibly, that somehow the Beast had overheard Rafe's conversation with his friends, over a year ago. "Is *that* what you've kept me here for?"

"I most sincerely doubt it," the Beast replied, sounding, indeed, most sincere. "Answer freely; it will cost you nothing."

I snapped, "Then don't be ridiculous," and stalked out.

I slept better than I would have expected, under the circumstances, and awoke the next morning so warm and comfortable that for a few breaths it was as if the fire had never happened and we had never left the city. Then memory returned, crushing those happy thoughts, and I rolled over to bury my face in the pillows and cry. When that was over, I forced myself out of bed to find eggs and toast and more of that glorious bacon awaiting me, which made it harder to be miserable. Once fed, I dressed in the most sensible clothes available to me, put on my amber necklace, and went exploring.

The library lay where I'd expected ballrooms to be, but in the opposite rounded facade my expectations were fulfilled: a magnificent ballroom, with balconies and seating areas unlike the library's, all open to the high ceiling rather than shaping the room like an egg. I wondered when the last time a ball had been held there, then went away from that room in hopes of finding answers to that, and other, questions.

The halls were broad with floors of well-polished parquet, and lit with candles that roused themselves when I came close, then went dormant again behind me. I opened innumerable doors, finding nothing more extraordinary than bedrooms and sitting rooms. I spent half a day doing that, walking far enough inside the palace that by lunchtime I was wobbling with exhaustion. The Beast didn't join me for lunch, and to my embarrassment, I fell asleep in front of the dining room fire only to be awakened by his arrival near dinnertime. "I've been working hard every day for over a year," I mumbled in apology. "I don't know why a walk around a house, even a big one, put me to sleep."

"Did your older sister sleep a lot after you arrived at the lodge?"

"Pearl has always slept a lot." I frowned at the Beast, trying to order my thoughts. "But now that you mention it, yes, she did. A great deal. So did Maman. I thought they were just grieving for the life we'd lost."

"That's no doubt part of it, but it often happens when magic awakens, and your sister had only just become a witch, hadn't she?"

"How do you *know* that?" I wasn't quite awake enough to be scared or angry by his knowledge, only befuddled by it.

"You live in my forest, and now in my palace. I know a great deal about what goes on here."

"Do the little birds and mice come to tell you?" I mumbled, scrubbing my hands over my face. "All right, if you don't want to tell me, don't. Have you eaten? Because I think I'm going to have dinner and go back to bed."

"I will keep you company."

"All right." From the way he'd said it, I thought if I flapped a hand at him and told him to shoo, that he would, which made me more willing to have him stay. Dinner was no less extravagant than it had been the night before, and I found myself breathing, "Are you sure you're not fattening me up?" without expectation of being heard.

"Quite sure. Judging from how much of the house you explored today, I think you're in no danger even if I was trying to." The Beast's mouth was not well suited to a smile, but I thought I saw a glimpse of one at its corner as I looked up guiltily. "I have excellent hearing," he offered, as if it was an apology.

"And probably a keen sense of smell," I muttered, but that time I expected to be heard.

His face twitched with amusement again. "Yes."

"What are you?"

I hadn't meant to ask that. The Beast's entire form went fierce with surprise and I quailed, more shocked by the asking than the response. It took a few seconds for either of us to be able to speak, and when he did, he replied, "A Beast," without any of the humor from before.

I set my teeth together. "Yes, but you weren't always, were you. A Beast who had never been a man wouldn't care about clothes, or what he looked like when he ate, or ancient libraries restored in his own. Or spy on a family in a hunting lodge nearby, and you did spy. You knew all of our names. You gave them that wagonload of goods. The cloth, the books, the *stones*. Why?"

"Most of the stones carry protective charms. The rest was as much to disguise their importance as anything else."

A chill sluiced down my spine and over my

arms. "Why do they need protection? And what do you mean, *most* of the stones?" I curled my fingers around the amber necklace I wore, wondering if it offered protection, and from whom. Or what, if it came to that.

The Beast, watching me, said, "It's woven with a protective charm as well. I wasn't sure if you'd wear it."

"It makes me feel closer to my family. Why are the stones all charmed?"

"Magic can be troublesome." The Beast shrugged a huge shoulder. "The pearl is more than just charmed, and could be of great help to your sister's witchery, if she chooses to use it."

"I could feel it had power. It made my hands tingle. Why wouldn't she use it?"

"Because she's received it in exchange for her sister."

"A bridewealth, paid to the whole family?"

The Beast held himself still for a breath, then released it in an exhalation that seemed even larger than he was. "I would not have said that. Since you've broached the topic, though, Amber, will you sleep with me?"

"For the Queen's sake, no! Are you going to ask me that every day? What use will the pearl be to Pearl? What can she use it for?"

"If she learns, you'll know." The Beast raised a paw. "Amber, there is very little I can tell you about...anything. I can tell you that I'm caught in a war between two very powerful and very angry people, and that I can do nothing directly to challenge my fate."

A dozen more questions leapt to my lips and stopped there, another chill draining through me. "'Directly'."

He nodded once, and I got up and left the table to chase the edges of understanding undisturbed.

The Beast was a pawn in a war. The idea of his great and terrible self being unable to guide his own fate carried twists of black humor: I, who was so much less than he — and arguably much more, being at least human — could hardly dream of managing my own future if the Beast couldn't direct his.

Could not *directly* affect his. But my sister was a witch, and he had given her a gift of magic. I had no doubt that was an indirect action that could affect him, if Pearl were to pursue it. I thought she would. The pearl had power, and I doubted the new-found witchery in her veins would let it lie. I didn't know what would happen then, but I had confidence in *something* happening.

I might be here only as an incentive, an excuse, to get that pearl to my sister. But perhaps there was more than that; perhaps my being here simply disrupted the status quo, changed the places of the pieces on the board, if nothing else. An extra piece had to change the game in some way. I found the idea oddly comforting. If there was some purpose to my captivity, then that captivity — not exactly onerous as it was — was easier to accept.

I had taken the stairs to my room. I was *certain* I had taken the stairs to my room, but my room was only a few steps down the corridor, and I had been walking for some time already. The palace had grown colder, as if the walls thinned and the wind came up to blow through them. I looked behind me, but the hall was gone: instead I looked at a courtyard, cobblestoned and walled with polished stone. Dirty, melting snow lay in cracks between the cobbles, but the air warmed, carrying the scent of spring rot in it.

A woman walked out of the walls, carrying a bundled infant in her arms. She was hooded in a green cloak embroidered at the hem with roses, and shook the hood back as she approached me, revealing a strongly-jawed round face and pale eyes with a ring of black around the irises. They made her expression intense, as did the hint of a sneer around her lips, as if anything I did was known to her and already harshly judged.

Then she smiled, and affection filled me, as well as loss. I embraced her and kissed the child, then swiftly turned away to mount a tall horse who wore the accoutrements of war. So did I, for that matter: chain mail that fit well, the weight of the cowl unfamiliar on my shoulders. More familiar was the sword at my hip and the leather, metal-knuckled gloves I gripped the reins with. I clicked at the horse, and we rode out of the courtyard to stand before an army of thousands, whose voices all rose as one as I came to them. A corridor opened through their center and I charged down it, letting their cheers propel me forward into war.

I fought like the mother sun who had been separated from her lover, the sister moon. I fought with the strength of grief and the resolution of sorrow. Every night I worked the spell I had been given by my lady, she who now watched over my infant son. Every night I kissed one of my husband's bones and buried it in the earth, dedicating his body to the huntress moon, and every morning I let three drops of my own blood fall where the bone had been, asking the brutal sun goddess to be our strength. Where my blood and his bones lay, a border rose, defining my kingdom so that none could ever again dare to claim it as their own. When there were no more bones to bury, I gave three drops of my blood to the huntress moon and six to her sister the sun, and built our border that way.

For three years I fought and bled and rode, until my enemy could run no more, and finally stood to face me. He had mocked my husband and then me, believing our goddess-worshiping country to be weak, and for his arrogance, died beneath my blade.

We rode home in triumph, my army and I, and I, Amber, found myself at the door of my room, as if I had never gone anywhere else. I flinched, whipping to search for the army, my horse, the scars on my fingers where I had bled and bled and bled again for my country, and none of it was there. I hurried into my room and poured wine that I hunched before the fire with, trying to clear my head of the visions. I fell asleep there, huddled around a glass of wine, and was grateful that the visions didn't pursue me into dreams.

Morning came early, and I awakened stiff and uncomfortable from sleeping on a rug. I groaned as I rolled over, and thought I heard a worried buzz from the invisible servants. "I wonder if you *could* have put me in bed," I said to their fussing.

The inaudible hum intensified. I creaked laughter and sat up. "I take it you couldn't, or thought you shouldn't. Well, if there's a next time, although I hope there isn't, you may. If you can."

Hairs stood up on my nape as they hummed at one another, or perhaps at me. Maybe they really couldn't lift a sleeping person from the floor. Maybe the only person in the palace who could was the Beast. My stomach turned over with nerves, and I concluded that invisible servants carrying me around were one thing but a Beast was something else entirely. "All right," I whispered. "Leave me on the floor, then. I'll try to get to bed next time, instead."

The inaudible hum faded, letting me relax. The clinking of china and glassware told me that a meal had appeared somewhere in the room, so I climbed to my feet and went to indulge, again, in crisp bacon. We hadn't had bacon at all since leaving the city, and it had never been this good. Enchanted bacon was a more prosaic use of magic than I had ever imagined, but one I entirely approved of.

I left my bedroom more apprehensively than I had the previous morning, as if the castle might aggressively besiege me with visions again. If, in fact, they had been visions at all: I had certainly known the story I'd been part of. It was the Queen's War, the one that had defined our country and staved off invasion so very long ago. I had *been* Queen Irindala in it, with the weight of a sword comfortable in my hand. No story I'd ever heard had told of the burying of the king's bones, though, or the blood sacrifice to build our kingdom's borders. But then, enchantment belonged to faeries or witches, and was considered suspect within our realm. Even if the queen was known to have witchy associates — and she was, else she would never have lived such an improbable span—she would not have been likely to confess to casting a spell, even to protect our borders.

My feet had taken me not to the breakfast room, but outside the palace. I looked up at it now, myself a small and solitary thing standing in the snow before its great edifice, and wondered at how long it had been there. It seemed that it must have stood since the Queen's youth, at least; it was as if the palace carried living memories of that time. *And* it had that library full of ancient, rescued books. Maybe the palace—or some version of it, at least—had been here always, collecting memories and stories that would otherwise be lost. Perhaps I could find my way into a corridor that would tell me of Boudicca, or one that would know the tale of the physician Al Shifa.

Maybe, a small and quiet part of me thought, maybe I could find a room that would let me know my long-dead mother, although Father still carried her memories with him, so perhaps they weren't lost enough for the palace's enchantments.

I was outside anyway, so I went past the frozen pools toward the gardens where so much trouble had begun. There were other fresh footprints in the snow: the Beast had come this way since the end of the storm. I put my foot into one of his prints and puffed a steamy breath of awe into the cold air. He'd been walking on all fours, which changed the shape of what pressed into the snow, but my foot still fit tidily into one of his paw prints. If he'd been walking upright I'd have been able to put both feet, heel to toe, into the print, and probably had room to spare.

The rose garden looked more gnarled than I remembered it from only a few days ago, but I hadn't been paying the closest attention, by the end of it all. I wandered its paths, rubbing my palm in memory of the prickles I'd taken, and did *not* pick any roses. After a while I went back to the library, where tea and scones with strawberry jam awaited me, and I wondered aloud if perhaps a book or two on perfumery might be found.

By the time I'd settled by the fire with my scones, a tidy stack of books and scrolls had arrived on the nearest table. I chose a scroll and unrolled it, then screwed my eyes shut as the text on it danced and swam. A second look rendered it perfectly readable, and I made a note to myself that I should probably always open a book and glance away briefly before trying to read it. Then I laughed. "How easily we adapt to enchantment, hm?"

The under-the-skin hum buzzed at that, and I smiled, this time apologetically. "I'm sorry. I didn't mean to make light of your situation." The scroll held a recipe for a perfume called *khemet*, made with cinnamon and myrrh and sweet wine, though the properties of the wine weren't described beyond its sweetness. I said, half to myself and half to the palace, "I don't suppose any of this particular sweet wine is lingering in the cellars," and put the scroll aside to examine others.

Nearly all of them contained recipes I didn't know, but many of those required ingredients I was confident of finding in the kitchen or on the grounds, come the thaw. I found myself talking to the library about them, explaining what I knew about how the scents combined, or the differences in practicality for a wax-based perfume versus a liquid one. I whiled away the afternoon in that pursuit, narrowing the scents I wanted to create—first, at least—down from dozens to three. I sighed contentedly and stacked the unneeded books together, thanking the servants as the books returned to their shelves one by one, and gathered the three I wanted to bring back to my room.

The khemet recipe scroll, which I thought I'd put away, wobbled at the edge of the table. Beside it stood a bottle no taller than my hand, so old that embedded dust had pitted the glass. My head snapped up and I looked around the room in astonishment, as if I could lay eyes on the servant who had delivered the little bottle. There was no one there, of course, so I picked the bottle up, gently tilting it to watch the wine inside shift. "Stars of earth and heaven. Thank you. How did you...thank you!"

My treasures clutched carefully in my arms, I left the library with a sense of satisfied servants in my wake.

I was late to dinner, and came down smelling of a peculiar enough array of herbs and spices that the Beast's nose twitched, though he didn't say anything. Dinner didn't taste quite right, either, with strong scents still clinging to my hands, even though I'd washed them with soap and then with lemon water. Eventually, as if testing uncertain waters, the Beast said, "You've found a way to entertain yourself?" and unleashed two or three hours of enthusiastic lecture on the topic of perfume-making. To his credit, he retained the appearance of interest, and it was only when my own stomach rumbled with a consideration of dessert that I realized the Beast had probably not eaten at all.

When the demand was put to him, he only shrugged. "I can eat later. It's been a long time since I've had anyone to converse with. Or," he amended, with what might have been the hint of a smile, "to converse *at* me."

"You should still eat," I said firmly, aware I sounded like Opal fussing over the boys when they were ill. "I'll look away, or pretend not to watch, but if I'm going to be here forever it's ridiculous for you to not have dinner with me."

The Beast gave me a measured look. "You are adapting very well."

"I believe I may be in some sort of denial." That was true enough: I couldn't really imagine remaining at the Beast's palace forever. Thinking about it, though, made it seem too real, so I added, more lightly, "Also, there are books. I've missed reading, the past year. Apple pie, perhaps?"

To my relief, the Beast responded with precisely the right amount of solemn pedantry: "I have never read an apple pie."

I smiled. "To eat. As an experimental meal shared. No one expects pie to be eaten tidily; it's too delicious."

The Beast, playing the role of pedant perfectly, said, "Ah," with only the gravest hint of humor, as if my explanation had been entirely necessary. I giggled beneath his continued, "I haven't had apple pie in…a very long time. My tastes run more toward the carnivorous. And I haven't had dinner."

"I might submit, Master Beast, that you are quite old enough to decide that once in a while, dessert might come before dinner." He cast a glance at me, and I, following with uncomfortably great precision where his thoughts ran, threw my palm off to stave off his words. "No. I am not dessert, and I won't sleep with you."

That time there was no doubt that the curl

of his lip indicated humor, as a low rumble of laughter rolled from his chest. "Then I suppose I'll have to try some apple pie."

Unexpectedly delighted, I clapped my hands together and said, "May we please have some apple pie?" to the room, which developed a sense of bustling off to do a job. "Can you feel it when they talk to each other? That buzz that settles under the skin?"

The Beast quirked an eyebrow and shook his head. "You do?"

"Obviously, or I wouldn't have asked. I wonder if you've gotten used to it, or if you're too magical yourself to notice."

"Perhaps," the Beast suggested dryly, "they don't talk to each other around me."

"Do you talk to them?"

His startled look was sufficient answer to the question. I said, "Well then," as if the problem was obvious, and by then an exceptionally large apple pie, easily two feet across, had arrived as the centerpiece on the table. A plate of ordinary proportions sat at my place, and a considerably bigger one had been placed where the Beast usually sat. "I don't think I can eat even one slice of that. Perhaps I could take a…dollop, and the rest can be yours to do with as you see fit."

"Thrust my face into, and slobber, perhaps," the Beast said, still dryly.

I looked up at him, genuinely curious. "Is that the best you can do?"

"It's not unlike what I usually do," he admitted. "I haven't tried eating like a civilized being for a long time."

"Since the last time you had apple pie, perhaps. Well, would you like to give it a try?"

"...not with an audience."

That seemed eminently fair. I nodded. "Maybe I'll just have a bit of pie, then, and leave you to your own devices."

The Beast turned his head away from me a little, as though I'd landed a blow I hadn't even meant to throw. "Why," he said again, "would you be kind to me?"

"I don't know," I also said again, and got myself some pie. It was delicious, full of cinnamon and cloves, and there was a custard to pour over the top. I ate my piece, thinking about his question, and finally said, "I suppose behaving nicely is as much for my own benefit as yours. Probably more. I could be angry and afraid," and even saying those words lit their fire inside of me, so I took a breath, trying to ease their burn. "But there's clearly very little I could do to harm you, which means feeding my anger is more likely to make *me* miserable than you. So I suppose I'm trying to let it go by being nice. It helps that aside from our first meeting, and the fact that you coerced me into staying..." I had to breathe again, trying to shake off the memory of fear and the still-vivid fury that those admissions acknowledged before I continued. "Aside from that, you've been...quite pleasant yourself."

"Aside from that," the Beast echoed. "As if those things could be pushed aside."

"Did you come here of your own volition?"

The Beast cast me a startled glance. "No."

"Would you leave if you could?"

"I would."

"Then you and I aren't so different, except I see my captor every day and I think you don't. I don't even know which is worse. As long as I see you every day, there might be a chance I could talk you into letting me go. If whomever put you here is long gone, you don't even have that chance. So if I'm kind, maybe it's because I hope it'll awaken a sympathetic kindness in you, and you'll release me."

"Rather than be angry, and hope your rudeness will drive me to send you away?"

"You're a Beast," I said with a degree of scathing that would do Pearl proud. "If I fight, your nature will make mastering me your prize, and no master ever wants to release his prize. Prizes are things, and things don't have feelings that matter. If I have any hope of getting out of here, it's in making you see me as a person. An equal. Someone worthy of respect. Maybe you won't. Maybe you can't. But making myself into a monster to earn that respect means you win anyway, so I'll be kind where I can be."

The Beast watched me through all of that speech, and when it ended, said, "It's possible

I've never respected anyone as much as I do you, in this moment. You're very wise, for one so young."

"But you're still not going to let me go."

"No."

"Fine. Enjoy your pie, Beast." I stalked from the dining hall, and managed not to cry until I was safely in my own rooms.

I only saw the Beast at the evening meal for the next several days. All he did, each evening, was ask me if I would sleep with him, and once denied, disappeared again. I told myself it was less offensive to be left alone than to be visited by a captor who had no intention of letting me go. That was true, but it was also lonelier. I worked on my perfumes—the khemet one took a month to brew, so I found other recipes and mixed them until my room was overwhelmed with scent—and I went out to glare at the gardens, and I talked to servants whom I could neither see nor understand, assuming the hair-raising subliminal muttering was indeed them.

As such, the days were difficult to track. I had been there a week before I thought to begin a calendar, and even that only came to mind because my blood began to flow. It made a way to mark the days, though, so I used it as the beginning of my calendar, and noted the phase of the moon—new, the sky hanging empty—to help remember the details of time's passage. It helped keep track of the perfume brews, too, so those three things became my points of reference: the moon, the blood, and the perfume.

The khemet was almost done when I arose one morning to go on my daily tromp around the gardens, and found a steady, drenching rain falling. All the snow was gone, and the earth, between blades of dead, yellow grass, looked saturated unto mud.

I had no doubt galoshes and oilskins would appear if I asked for them, or even if I simply rooted around in the wardrobe for a while, but the prospect of going out into the rain was too depressing. At home, Opal and Flint, especially, would be pleased by its offering the first hint of spring, and at the softening of the ground. They wouldn't yet be planting seeds, but they might turn the earth over, helping it to thaw, while Pearl muttered curses about dirty feet and hard labor. Or perhaps they were only awaiting spring because it could offer—with the goods the Beast had sent with Father—the chance to return to the city, and begin a more luxurious life all over again.

My heart faltered at the thought. It was one thing to be captive in a castle at the heart of an enchanted forest that my family lived in, no matter the distance. Somehow it was something else entirely to not even share the forest's borders with them. Distressed and trying to shake it off, I wrapped myself in a warm cloak and went for a walk inside the palace, which was large enough to exercise horses in, never mind one young woman. I wasn't looking where I was going; escape from my own thoughts, not exploration, was my purpose.

So it took longer than it might have otherwise to realize that the parquet beneath my feet had turned to smooth road, and then that I had sometime recently stopped walking, and now rode astride a familiar charger. I patted the creature's neck, feeling callouses from a sword marring my palm, and looked ahead to see the great gates of my city rising before me. The road became cobblestones, and I rode home at the head of my army, the triumphant warrior queen returning. I had gone to war bearing my husband's standard; now I carried my own, a blazing sun, crowned and crossed behind by a sword and a needle, so that no one might mistake my symbol for a man's. Among the crowds were thousands of women waving needlework, an honor that delighted me; I raised my blade and named it the Needle, for them, and their roars of pride carried me all the way to the palace.

At its gates I could — or did, at least, whether I should or not — shed the persona of queen, and instead became the mother I had missed being for three full years. The same woman, clad in gold this time instead of green, but still with her beloved roses embroidered at the hem, came forth with her sweet, wicked smile. With her walked a little boy whose eyes were large and round with awe. I slipped from my horse and knelt, my arms open, and he did not run to me. Instead he clung to the gold woman's skirts, and a whisper of sympathy rippled behind me as my soldiers saw what happened.

I ought to have known: a good leader doesn't fight a losing battle in public, not if she can help it. But I hadn't thought it through; I had forgotten that a mother's longing over a three-year campaign would not be reflected in the heart of a child who had barely been off the breast when his mother left. Nell was my sweet boy's mother, for all that he knew or cared, and I would damage us all if I tried to change that in an instant. So I stood, still smiling, hoping that smile's cost didn't show, and embraced Nell as she came to me. The little boy in her skirts watched me, and when Nell made as if to encourage him to hug me, I shook my head just a little. One rejection in front of the troops was enough. More than enough.

Nell, who was wise, lifted him onto her hip, and stood beside me so he was between us both, and we turned to face my army, crying, "Your prince!"

The roar of approval made my son gasp,

then hide his face in Nell's shoulder, and, finally, peek out and smile, to the chortling delight of the army. When the tales of that day came to me in later years, they were told the way I had hoped it would go: that the little prince had run to me, and we faced our troops together, with Nell, my strong right hand, at our side. It made a better story, but I knew it was only that, and so that night, as soon as I had a moment alone with her, I said to my Nell, "I owe you a debt that can never be repaid. He loves you," and Nell, smiling, said, "I love him too."

It wanted to be a festering wound, that my son went to Nell for comfort and laughter. I wouldn't let it: I could not hate she who had held the kingdom for me for so long, nor could I blame him for not knowing a mother who had left him behind. Nell, generous of heart, saw my struggle, and guided him toward me, little by little. "What does it cost you," I asked late one night, and she only shrugged, stroking my hair.

"I never wanted children, unless I could beget one on you. Your son is as close as I can have to that, but he's *your* son. I was never more than a caretaker to him." Her stroking fingers made their way down my belly and thighs, until I, Amber, came to myself shuddering with pleasure and leaning on a windowsill for support.

Night had fallen and the rain had stopped

while I'd been tangled in Irindala's...dreams. I had no better word for what they were. My dreams, perhaps, and her memories, but whichever they were, they'd stolen the day away from me. Flushed, I went to wash before dinner, and to my surprise, then found the dining hall empty. I had no sense of the time at all, save that I was hungry, but the Beast had always waited for me before. I ate a little, then, remembering it, went to the observatory to see if the height of the moon might tell me if I'd lost more than the day, but also half the night as well.

I knew before I climbed the observatory's narrow stairs that the Beast was up there: the air's weight changed when he was nearby, and in daylight or at dinner I had become largely accustomed to it. It felt different at night, without the familiar trappings, and I noticed it more clearly. Nor did it fade as I entered the observatory. It was late indeed, the stars so far along in their nightly wheel that morning had to be closer than dusk. The Beast was a shadow on the floor. I barely had time to realize he was lying on his back, belly exposed to the sky like a giant dog, before he flipped himself over and rose to his feet with inhuman speed. "Amber?"

"Did I wake you?" Amusement colored my

tone. I couldn't imagine him being caught in such an undignified position unless he hadn't heard or smelled me coming, and I doubted he would fail to do either of those things unless he had been asleep.

He sounded gruffly embarrassed. "Yes."

"Sorry." I sat on one of the cushioned benches, looking up at the stars. "Do you often sleep up here?"

"Often enough," he said guardedly. "I find the distance from the gardens comforting."

"The gardens," I echoed, faintly surprised. "It's the forest that seems threatening, to me."

"And yet it was the roses that imprisoned you here."

I glanced at him, an eyebrow arched. "The *roses*?"

"The edict that they must not be picked is not mine. I only enforce it."

"With great enthusiasm. Does this place— does it drag you into visions, too? Memories so real it's like you're living them yourself?"

The Beast bared his teeth suddenly, a brief and ferocious gesture. My gut tightened, but his gaze turned away; apparently the anger he'd shown wasn't for me. "No. Not for a long time."

"That's your answer to everything!"

"That is my experience." He sat on the bench opposite me, as well away from me as he could in the confines of the observatory. I thought he was trying not to trap me, which would have been comforting if he hadn't continued in a low growl. "This place, this palace…it rescues stories. It's trying to determine how you fit into its story. Where you belong. What role you play."

I drew my knees up, looking to the stars again. "What role *do* I play?"

The Beast shook his head. "I don't know. I'm an old part of its story, now. The captive in the castle. But there is rarely more than one captive in the old tales, Amber, so by rights, you must play some other role. It's trying on its memories, the stories that it knows, to see if any of them fit you."

"Why is it telling me Queen Irindala's story?"

A truly massive sound of surprise erupted from the Beast's chest. "Irindala was my mother."

I made an incredulous sound almost as large. "But you're a Beast! Irindala only had one child, the son who was los—oh. *Oh.*" I stared across the darkness at him, dumbfounded. "I knew you weren't always a Beast. How stupid of me."

"Oh yes." The Beast shifted on the bench, folding himself until he lay like an enormous cat, his front feet folded neatly over one another, and looked toward me levelly. "How stupid of you to not immediately realize that the monster who took you captive was in fact the queen's son who disappeared over a century ago. Whatever could you have been thinking."

"Why didn't you tell me?"

He took a breath that expanded his apparent size by half, and exhaled it in something near a growl. "Would you have believed me?"

I spread my hands, trying to encompass everything: the palace that shouldn't be there, the Beast lying before me, the servants who were invisible but extraordinarily good at procuring whatever might be desired at a moment's notice, and said, "Probably."

The Beast chuffed, the deep sound I was coming to recognize as his laughter, and dipped his head in a nod. "Perhaps you would have. I think it didn't occur to me. People rarely find their way here, and I encounter few of those who do. Much of my time is spent…" He moved a paw as a cat might twitch its tail, or a human wave a hand, as if trying to say something words didn't easily convey.

"As a Beast?" I ventured. "Without thought, without…time?"

"It was sheer fortune that I wore trousers when I first saw you," he said, as if that supported my theory. I supposed it did, at that, but it made me smile anyway. "I hadn't bothered with any kind of…humanity…for—" His gaze lifted suddenly and I said it for him, amused: "A long time."

"Quite a long time indeed," he agreed. "If I'd

been more in practice I might have been less…"

"Terrifying," I offered. "Loud. Monstrous. Rabid. Enrag—"

"That," the Beast said prissily, "is quite enough. But yes. All I knew was that someone had picked a rose, and I was furious. It took me most of the way to the garden to remember how to use words."

"You succeeded admirably, in the end. Loudly. Viciously. Frighteningly. But admirably."

He gave me a look that really did remind me wonderfully of Pearl. "Must you?"

"I'm beginning to think I must. How did you end up a Beast?"

"Ah," he said, softly. "That I can't tell you."

"You don't know?"

"I can't tell you. Like the picking of a rose, like the—" He stopped himself suddenly, then began again. "There are things that must and must not be done, here. Telling the entirety of my story is one of them."

"But why?"

"Amber. I am a Beast in an enchanted castle in a forest. What other answer do you expect?"

"Well, there must be some way to tell me."

He sighed. "The enchantment will tell you, if you wander the deeper parts of the palace unguarded. The main hall, the dining room and kitchen, our bedrooms, they're safe enough, but beyond them…" His tremendous shoulders rolled in a shrug. "You should know, though, Amber...the magic will want to make you a part of its story. To make you fit into the roles it already knows. And it will try to kill you, if it fails."

"Stars of earth and fire," I said as mildly as I could. "Has that happened often?"

The Beast rose, a dark and dangerous shadow against the starlight. "More than once."

He paced toward the stairs, clearly intending to leave me alone with the weight of that information. I waited until distance had nearly taken him, then said, "Beast. We missed dinner together, so you had better ask me now. Because you have to, don't you? It's one of those *musts*."

He turned his head back, though we could never make eye contact in the darkness. "Amber, will you sleep with me?"

"What would happen if I said yes?"

"I don't exactly know."

"So no one ever has."

His low laugh rolled across the room toward me. "No. No one ever has. The last person I was obliged to ask was perhaps the most beautiful person I have ever laid eyes upon. Perfect, a pure paragon. He...did not take the request well."

I murmured, "Oh dear," and then more clearly, but measuredly, wondering what the cost of either answer would be, said, "No, Beast, I won't sleep with you."

He bowed his head. "I thought not. Good night, Amber."

I said, "Good night, Beast," and he left me alone in the dark.

I stayed in my room most of the next day, working on perfumes and—I knew this perfectly well—avoiding any possibility of the enchantment drawing me down a hallway and trying to fit me into a predestined place. I emerged for dinner, which the Beast, very cautiously, took with me. I accused him of having been practicing eating like a civilized person, and he allowed that he may have been, and the evening passed in a strangely pleasant manner, even up unto the asking and answering of the ritual question. I didn't press him for any further details about the castle, the enchantment, or the paragon who had not cared to be propositioned by a Beast, and retired to bed early.

Dawn seemed to come even earlier, tenacious golden glow prying through my eyelids. I pulled a pillow over my head, determined to sleep a little longer, but heard someone repeating my name with increasing urgency. It wasn't the Beast, so I thought I had to be dreaming, as the servants had no audible voices and there was no one else to talk to. Finally, though, my oldest sister's voice sharpened unmistakably, and I bolted out of bed to her snapped, "*Amber!*"

Sunrise was coming from my vanity. Not reflected in it, but coming from it: the room's increasing brilliance shone from mirror's amber casing, and the mirror itself had taken on a silvery light of its own. I lurched to it, hardly awake enough to focus. My own tangle-haired reflection was barely visible in it, but Pearl, with her white hair cut short again so it was a cap of flyaway curls, looked out at me as though she sat five steps away, not across half an enchanted forest. "Oh, stars of heaven and earth, there you are. I've been hissing at you for half an hour."

"*Pearl?*" I sat heavily on my vanity stool, too thick-headed to comprehend what I saw. "Pearl, is that really you?"

"Of course it is. Keep your voice down. The family are all sleeping."

"What are you…how are you…?"

"I'm a witch, and I'm fine, thank you." Her familiar pedantry made me laugh, but I put my head down on the vanity table suddenly, overwhelmed with seeing her and not wanting to shed tears. Her voice softened unexpectedly. "We're all right, Amber. Are *you*?" I lifted a hand, trying to indicate a yes, and she went on, still more gently than I expected from my austere older sister. "That Beast paid well for you. The pearl he sent is a focus. I knew it had power the moment I touched it, but it's taken me this long to understand it well enough to contact you. I couldn't do it without the full moon. The ocean bends to the moon's pull, and the pearl is a prize of the sea. Its power waxes and wanes, but even in the dark of the moon it's a focus like nothing I've ever imagined."

By then I'd recovered myself enough to raise my head again, and even to smile at Pearl's enthusiasm. "Witchery suits you."

A pale gleam came into her eyes. "With a little more time, I think I can cast an enchantment to free you, Amber. Can you hold on there a little while longer?"

"Yes, but I don't think you can—" I cut myself off, remembering the Beast's inability to directly affect his fate, but his confidence that Pearl's magic would have an indirect effect. My sister, pale eyebrows elevated, waited for me to finish, and I spoke more slowly, trying to think out what the Beast had implied. "He knew you would discover its magic. He had faith in you."

"In *me*? How could he—" She stopped herself just as I had, muttering, "Obviously he knew us all, or he'd have never sent these particular jewels and stones. Maman has worn hers since the day it arrived, just over her heart. What does he expect me to do?"

"I don't know. The enchantment here is dreadfully powerful, Pearl. Whatever you do, don't rush it."

"Me." Pearl smiled faintly. "When have I

ever rushed anything, Amber?"

"Never. Oh, Pearl, it's so good to see you. How are the boys? How is Glover? Has Opal noticed him yet? Is Father all right? I miss you all so much." A tightness constricted my chest, crushing further questions a way.

A suspicious glimmer shone in Pearl's eyes, but she wouldn't lift a finger to dash tears away. "The boys are strong and healthy. Jasper has grown four inches since you've seen him, Amber, and Flint's voice is changing. Jet has an opinion on everything and gets elbow deep in dirt whenever he has the chance. Opal was well on the way to noticing Glover before Father returned without you. She's been…well, you know how Maman often is? Faded? Opal has become more like that than I'm happy with, and even Daniel can't bring her out of it."

"Daniel?"

"Daniel Glo—oh. Glover. His forename is Daniel." Pearl, for the first time in her life that I could recall, looked vaguely ashamed. "I never knew, until I heard Opal use it. Now we all call him Daniel."

"It's a fine name. And Father?"

Pearl's voice lowered. "Worse than Opal. He can't forgive himself for leaving you there, although the way he tells the tale, I'm not certain he had much choice."

"He didn't. Pearl, can you waken him? So he can see that I'm all right?"

"I don't know if more than one of us can use

the pearl. You told him!" she said, suddenly more acerbic and more herself. "You told him I was a witch."

"It came up," I said, hardly remembering how. "Has he taken it all right?"

"He hasn't fought me on it, if that's what you mean. He's taken nothing well since he came home, though. He feels guilty."

"Wake him up," I said firmly. "He needs to see I'm all right."

"*Are* you? The Beast sounded..." Pearl faltered, obviously uncertain what words would sufficiently describe my captor.

I nodded. "And he is. But he's more than that, and I don't even understand all of it yet myself. I'll be all right, Pearl, I swear it. But please, let Father see that I am. At least let us try."

She nodded and stood, climbing the stairs without releasing the pearl. I heard her whisper his name, and could see from how my field of vision moved that she shook him. He awakened with a concerned grunt, and I heard explanatory murmurs before she sat beside him on the edge of the bed, and his face, with hers in the periphery, swam into focus. He had aged visibly, more than just the old careful dye job having fully grown out. He looked thinner, paler, in a way the moonlight didn't account for. "Amber?"

"It's me, Father. I'm all right." Tears spilled over my smile. "I'm fine. Pearl says you've been worried. You don't have to worry, Papa. The Beast and I are getting on reasonably well, and I'm fine."

"How can you get along well with that monster?" His hoarse voice cracked, tears shimmering in his eyes.

"He's better tempered when someone hasn't just stolen his roses." I tried to loosen the tightness in my chest with a deep breath, and failed. "Is it still alive?"

"It's putting out roots," Father said bitterly. "Opal tends it, and Daniel says it should go in the ground soon. Your mother won't touch it, and neither will I."

"Perhaps it will thrive as long as I do," I said, then regretted it as Father's face pinched. "I intend to thrive a long time, Father. The Beast makes no demands of me. We usually dine together."

"How can that thing eat in a civilized manner?"

I breathed, "Awkwardly," and thought better of trying to offer further solace. "I'm so glad to see you, Father. I wish I could see all of you."

"Next time," Pearl promised. "At the next full moon. We'll have the whole family awake, now that we know it works."

"It will give me something to look forward to," I promised. "Tell everyone I love them, please?"

"We will." Their image blurred, and Pearl

cast a sharp look toward the window. "There are clouds coming in. They may affect the spell. If it's cloudy the next full moon, Amber —"

"I'll wait for all three nights of it," I said. "And if we miss that one, there will always be another. I love you. I love you!" The last words were cried as murkiness swept my mirror, and I heard nothing in response. I buried my face in my hands, dragging great gasping breaths, and only dared lift my head again when I was sure I had conquered tears.

The reflection in my mirror showed a woman, not just the girl I had been when Father and I had left the hunting lodge together three months ago. I didn't know exactly what the changes were: some roundness lost from my cheeks, perhaps, and a hollowness in my throat that hadn't been there before. Mostly, though, I thought it was my eyes. In the moonlight, their hazel tint took on a greener shade, though by daylight, with the mirror's amber frame, I thought they looked uncomfortably yellow. Like a beast's eyes, though not like *the* Beast's, whose beady gaze was as brown as any boar's. I preferred the green, even if there seemed to be a new understanding of sorrow in my reflection. I rose and found a robe, drawing it around myself as I went to the room's balcony.

Two days' worth of rain had stopped sometime while I slept, and though clouds had come to obscure Pearl's moon, here the night was bright. The forest had a malevolent, creeping sense to it beneath the blue night, though I doubted our grounds had diminished any.

Our. A moment's defense of the Beast to my father, and suddenly the palace was *ours*, not *his*. But then, we were its only two denizens, and unless Pearl's magic worked some rare witchery indeed, I didn't expect to be going anywhere any time soon. So ours it would be, if only in my thoughts. I brushed water from a balcony seat and settled into it, drawing my feet up off the cold floor.

Pearl was not the person in my family I would have imagined as the savior of a captive in a castle. Jasper, of all of us, seemed most suited to the role: I could see him, even at seven years old, brandishing a blade and fighting his way through brambles to rescue a lost soul. But the lot had fallen to Pearl, whose arrogance was at least matched by her intelligence; if we had to depend on someone to rescue us, there were worse choices. Particularly since Pearl would take failure as a personal affront, and the last time she'd been thwarted, with Solindra Nare, it had wakened in her a witchery none of us had dreamed slumbered within. If she was stymied in her first attempt at freeing me, I half expected her to take on the guise of a faery queen, and wreak havoc on the forest and palace alike.

Comforted by the thought, I drifted, half asleep beneath the moon, until my legs relaxed enough that my feet fell down and hit the cold floor, and I yelped and ran for bed.

True sunrise wakened me a few hours later. I felt lighter than I had in weeks, buoyed by having spoken with Pearl and Father. I wasn't sure, if I reflected on it, that I believed rescue was at hand, though certainly Pearl *would* orchestrate it if she could. My exile simply seemed less onerous, with the prospect of talking to and even seeing my family every month. It wasn't the same as feeling their warm embraces, but neither was I so alone anymore.

Strangely enough, that fact made me feel more sociable, even if the only soul I had to socialize with was the Beast. I ate a breakfast of toast and jam, foregoing the bacon as an act of willpower that I immediately questioned. The servants appeared to question it as well, as a small plate of bacon waited for me on a windowsill outside my room when I left it. I said, "Well, if you insist," and took the plate with me as I went in search of the Beast.

He haunted none of the spots I might expect him to: the dining hall, its parlor, the library, even the garden, which still squelched with standing water and mud, were abandoned. I knew where his rooms were, but was reluctant to go to them, not because I thought I would be unwelcome. No, I was afraid if I went beyond the main hall, the palace would guide me away from my intended destination and pull me into one of its stories, and I was not quite prepared to face another intimate history lesson.

The Beast was Irindala's son, the prince of our realm. I knew his *name*. I shied away from that knowledge, hardly even letting myself remember it. I'd asked him his name once, and he had accepted *Beast* in its stead. It seemed a trespass to go beyond that, even if he had since confessed — in effect if not in actuality — to what his name was. To pull myself away from those thoughts, I let myself into the other round-faced hall, the ballroom whose basic form echoed the library's. I hardly expected to find the Beast there, but it was the only other place in the palace that I was willing to go that I hadn't yet looked in.

Sunlight poured in through the enormous windows and reflected off the golden parquet floors, brightening the room far more than the library with its carpets and shelves could ever manage. A crystal chandelier hung far above me, singing gently as the door's opening and closing pushed a faint breeze through the hall. I stood beneath it, smiling upward at the rainbows it cast, and tried to imagine this room full of music and flirtation and laughter.

I should not have: I knew it almost as soon as the fancy touched me. Memory snatched at me, memory that was not my own. The room filled with indistinct figures, beautifully dressed; music played as if from a distance, a ghostly remove that made its tune lighter and sweeter than any I'd ever heard. I was swept into the steps of a dance, moving with comfortable confidence as I smiled at my partners. I was hardly anyone, a courtier with a pretty dress and an excellent bosom, and no one could tell me any different. But I could charm, and I could flirt, and I wasn't surprised when, between dances, a slim and handsome young man crossed the floor toward me.

Other men might have to work their way through the crowd. For this youth, the crowd parted just a little, just enough, and did it without conscious effort or awareness: the prerogative of royalty. He stopped before me, offering a hand and unleashing a devastating smile that begot a breathless laugh from me as I took his hand. He drew me close, pulling me into the dance, and I could hardly do more than gaze up at him in half-stunned admiration. He favored his mother in beauty, though he had the broad nose I'd seen in paintings of the long-dead king, and he wore his tightly curling black hair cropped close to his scalp the way his father had. But he had Irindala's wide bright smile, played up against sepia skin darker than hers, and a jaw meant for sculpting. His hands were soft and, I saw, stained with ink: a scholar prince rather than a warrior. But then, he was young, and Irindala hadn't gone to war until she was in her twenties. He smiled again, and I smiled in return, lost in his dark eyes.

The music changed, gaining in tempo, until it became something I had never heard before. The prince's smile faded as his concentration increased: trying not to step on my skirt or my feet, trying not to crush me as he kept pace with the dance. Then even concentration faltered, becoming alarm, though it seemed only he shared that concern: my heart flew with excitement, my breath coming in laughs and joy filling me as we tangled more tightly together. He tried to break away and couldn't, though my grip hardly seemed strong enough to keep him. Faster and faster we whirled, until the part of me that didn't belong in that story spun loose and *I* began to fear, though the pretty girl I embodied still laughed and thrilled with delight. Nor could *I* loosen my hold on the prince: we spun together, increasingly out of control, our breath burning in our bodies and sickness rising from the relentless twirling, the impossible pace. My feet began to hurt and tears started to leak from my eyes, but the woman who had started the dance loved every moment of it.

I came to a sudden, shocking stop, and the memory ripped away in a whirlwind of fear.

"Amber." The Beast was there, his massive paw at my waist, holding me. Catching me. Stopping me. My heart lurched in surprise and gratitude and something else that left my stomach hollow. I put my hand on his chest to steady myself and found, to my surprise, that I was trembling. I put my forehead against his chest—well, his ribs; he stood much too tall for me to reach his chest, really—and he sank to his haunches, lowering himself until he merely loomed over me, rather than towered. He put his other hand against my hair, the barest touch of reassurance. For all of his size, I *felt* reassured, not trapped, and stood there, drawing tremulous breaths and noticing his musky scent, until my shaking stopped.

"What was that," I finally whispered, and felt his massive head shake above mine.

"Dancing," he said. "Dancing is rarely safe in faery tales. Are you all right?"

"No." I shook my head, fingers coiled in the heavy mane that fell down his chest. "No. That was...was it trying to kill me, Beast?"

"To subsume you, I think. It's still searching for a place you can belong. But if I hadn't come..." He shook his head again. "You were careening around the room. There's not much in it to hurt yourself on, but in time you would have managed anyway."

I stepped back a little, looking up at him. Up: even settled on his haunches he was taller than I, if not by much. "How did you know to find me?"

He lifted my amber necklace off my breast with the tip of one careful claw. "I told you it has a protective charm. I felt it struggling to keep you safe, and came to help."

I closed my hand over the necklace, and over his fingers as well. "You felt it?"

"There's very little that goes on in this palace that I'm unaware of, and the necklace is part of the palace. It's all bound together, me and it."

"And me?"

The Beast shifted his big head, not quite a shake. "Not so tightly."

"And what about the things you sent to my family? Are they irrevocably bound up in this too?"

"Everything inside the forest's boundaries is, to one degree or another. The enchantment's influence lessens, the farther from the palace it goes. But you need not worry." What passed for his smile pulled at his mouth. "The coin is real enough, and won't turn to lead in the city. Nor will the books turn to dust, or the jewels to ordinary stones. Are you all right now?"

I took a shuddering breath and straightened my shoulders. "I think so."

He leaned forward, onto all fours. "I'll leave you, then."

"Don't!" I put a hand over my mouth as if I could block the blurted word too late, but said, "Don't," again, more quietly. "I'd rather not be alone. I don't...I don't trust the palace. I don't want to get caught in another story right now."

The Beast ducked his vast head, an invitation, and, emboldened, I curled my fingers into the thick fur along his spine, and walked from the ballroom with him.

"Does the palace...listen?" It had taken me until evening to gather the courage to ask, after a quiet day spent in the Beast's company. We had read in the library — or I, at least, had read, while the Beast had stretched out in front of the fire and napped like the beast he was — and taken dinner together, in so far as the Beast was willing to sit with me while I dined; he still wouldn't eat in my presence. Neither reading nor eating had been entirely able to take away the memory of the dance, or the beauty of the prince I'd danced *with*.

I could see absolutely nothing of him in the Beast, save perhaps a shared coloring. The Beast was dark-furred as the prince had been dark-skinned, but since every beast I saw in him, from lion to bear to boar, could be or habitually was darkly furred, that seemed more coincidence than reflection of who he had once been. I wanted to ask what *his* memory of that dance was, but it hadn't been memory, not all of it. It had been a vision, one I lacked the knowledge to fully understand, and I was afraid that if I pressed it, the palace would retaliate.

The Beast looked up at my question, great brows furrowing. Feeling foolish, I tried to explain myself. "I know the servants listen, obviously, but you said there are things you can't tell me. Does the palace listen? Is that how it knows what's being said?"

"Ah. No. The enchantment—" He gestured at his throat. "Seizes me, if I say too much. The palace doesn't have ears, but the magic has limits. If I come up against them, I pay the price."

I closed my lips on burgeoning questions. A shadow crossed the Beast's face. "I'm sorry I can't explain."

"It's all right. I'd rather you could stop me from dancing myself to death than explain, if it comes down to it. But if the palace doesn't listen—is it safe to tell you something, Beast?"

"I hope it is always safe for you to tell me whatever you wish, Amber."

"It has to do with Pearl's witchery," I said cautiously.

The Beast's ugly face lit up, his gaze sharpening on me. "Has she learned to use the pearl?"

"She's starting to. She spoke to me, Beast. Through my mirror, last night. They're all well." My heart soared, remembering the conversation. "Upset at my absence, but mostly well. I found myself defending you to them."

"Really. That—I would not have expected

that. Thank you. Which mirror?"

"The big one on my vanity. Why," I asked lightly, "does the other mirror do something too?"

He gave me a look that sent a flush of excitement through me, then twitched his head in a denial as I took breath to ask more. I bit my tongue, gazing at him and trying to remember what he'd told me about Pearl and her pearl. That it had power and she could use it, no more. He had been circumspect, and now I understood he may have been pushing the boundaries of what he was allowed to say about the enchantments here. I thought the same thing was happening now, and swallowed down my questions. I would have to explore for myself, although stars knew I lacked Pearl's native gift.

Then again, so had Pearl, before she'd been jilted. Perhaps I only needed the offense of being throughly rejected by a lover to waken magic in me.

The idea made me laugh aloud, surprising me and the Beast both. "I'm sorry," I said merrily. "I was imagining myself a witch. It didn't work very well. One in the family is enough. More than enough. I can almost hear our city neighbors clucking about it."

"And what would they say about the youngest daughter absconding to an enchanted castle?"

"That I had always been peculiar and that

you could never trust my smile anyway."

The Beast tilted his head, examining the smile that came with the pronouncement. "It's an inviting smile," he said after a moment. "Difficult to look away from."

"There you go," I said. "Witchery, no doubt."

"No doubt," the Beast replied solemnly.

I smiled at him again, then stood, stretching. "I suppose I should go to bed." In truth, I wanted to examine my little mirror and see if I could discover any magical properties, but he had ended that conversation, so admitting as much seemed gauche.

"I suppose you should." He watched me as I went to the door, and then, inevitably, said, "Amber, will you sleep with me?"

I looked back at him, one hand on the door frame, and thought of his protective hand on my waist in the ballroom earlier, and of the tremendous paw cradling my hair while I trembled. And I thought, because I could do nothing else, of his enormous size, nearly three feet taller than I, and of the beast-like proportions and angles that made up his body. "Beast," I said softly, "how would that even work?"

He murmured, "Indeed," and I left the room.

The mirror, to my disappointment, absolutely did not work with moonlight. I brought it to the balcony, filling its pane with blue-white light, and felt nothing. I polished it, rubbed its back, said silly chants, and accomplished nothing. Nor did I know what I expected to accomplish, save that the Beast implied something could be done with it. I gave up and went to bed, and in the morning, watching sunlight glow through the amber frame, chided myself for a silly goose and tried again.

It answered to my wish and to sunlight as it hadn't done with the moon. Well, of course: a pearl had all the properties of the moon, pale and luminous, with shadows in its depths. Amber was the very color of the sun, rich and gold and made of life itself, born from the scars of trees fighting to live on.

It was not, though, as powerful as Pearl's magic. The mirror's surface shimmered gold and cleared to show me little Jet studiously smearing handsful of mud all over his face, while beside him an adult's shadow dug at the earth. I cried out, but neither of them heard me. The adult stood, then stooped to collect Jet, and for a moment I saw Opal's laughing face, but couldn't hear her words or the joy in her voice as she spoke to my littlest brother. They looked happy, though, and I closed my eyes against the image, feeling both relieved to see them and saddened that the contact wasn't as intimate as Pearl's magic made it. I had felt like I was with them, then; watching through my mirror made me feel that much more removed. I would rather be fully *here*, with the Beast, than pretending at a half-life of my family, whom I could only see and not hear or touch.

The image swam, then focused again, this time to show me the Beast. He, with the innocence of one who had no idea he was being watched, sat on his haunches and lifted his back leg to scratch at his mane. I yelped, embarrassed to have caught him in such an undignified pose, and pressed the mirror's surface against my chest so I wouldn't see any more. A moment later I peeked again, but I saw only my own amused face reflected back at me. "Very well," I said, both to my reflection and myself, "this mirror is not for me, unless I wish to go into the Queen's service as a spy, and learn to read lips."

The mirror blurred again. I put it down swiftly, its face against the vanity, rather than see what my commentary might awaken in its surface. I didn't *want* to become the Queen's spy, or risk any method of contacting her; explaining that I was the latest captive at her son's enchanted palace was beyond me, and I had an itching conviction that she would somehow be able to reach through the mirror's limitations and force those confessions from me.

"Which is madness," I breathed, but then again, I lived in an enchanted castle, and what seemed like madness on the surface might be perfectly reasonable when that surface was scratched.

"Perfumes," I said to myself, and resolutely stood to check my mixtures and their scents, testing them for strength and potency. Some of them wanted rose water, and what little I had had left after the city was all but gone. I gathered a cloak and, at the insistent murmuring of the invisible servants, a scone, and went out to the gardens.

The roses, which had never stopped blooming, had grown ferocious in the oncoming spring sunshine, and now covered the garden walls in relentless color. Loose petals drifted to the ground on every breath of wind, until a carpet of color greeted my feet. I began gathering the petals in my skirt as they fell, determined to use them in rose water: I would have my perfume yet, even if the garden didn't like me picking its roses.

Behind me, and without warning, the Beast said, "I believe you're safe enough picking them now that you're a guest here."

I shrieked and spasmed, narrowly keeping my grip—and thus my collected petals—in my skirt. "Could you please make some *noise*!"

"Evidently not. Are you all right?"

"Fine, save for a heart seizure!" I glowered at the Beast, who failed to look at all threatened.

Piqued, I pulled a rose from one of the bushes, and aside from a piercing pain where I hadn't been careful enough of the thorns, suffered no ill effects. "Why didn't you tell me I could pick them?"

"I didn't know you wanted to."

"How maddeningly reasonable." I turned my palm up, examining a startling well of blood from the thorns. "I don't think the roses like me. Does this look strange to you?" The Beast hesitated, but I thrust my hand at him, displaying the blood rising from it. "It's got a golden sheen," I insisted. "It happens every time one of those thorns gets me."

He sat on his haunches like an enormous dog and lifted one paw to not quite cup my hand. I still felt his body heat, tremendous compared to my own, and resisted the impulse to settle my hand in his and feel if the pads of his palm were as rough as they looked. "Perhaps," he said after a careful look. "My eyesight isn't what it might be, but you may be right."

I'd quite forgotten about my injury by then, so intently was I studying him from so close. He was nearly as tall as I, sitting as he was, and I could see the short, velvet-like fur on his nose. It stretched into longer tufts at the bridge, thickening to a visible depth over the brow ridges before lengthening into the coarse mane that only parted around the twisting horns that swept back from his forehead.

"Where are your ears?"

The Beast drew his head back, focusing on me with apparent effort. "My ears?"

"I assume you have them. But they're not... where they belong. Bears, boars, lions, goats, antelope...everything you remind me of has ears up here." I gestured vaguely along the outer lines of his forehead and skull, where animals tended to keep their ears. "Where are they?"

Moving slowly, and still watching me as though I had perhaps lost my mind, the Beast sat all the way back on his haunches and pawed through his mane until he'd exposed an ear far more human than animal, though it swept into a pointier tip than any human had ever sported. It struck me as delicate and unsuitable for his enormous rough form. "Well. You have lovely ears."

The Beast's laughter, from this close, shook the petals of my rose. "Do I?"

"Very. And if your eyesight is poor, I think they would support glasses very nicely. Have you ever asked the servants for any?"

His incredulous look said he had not. "My face is hardly shaped for them."

"If we trimmed this up," I said, not quite touching the longer fur at the bridge of his nose, "I think they might work fairly well. And this only needs trimming so the glasses don't push the fur into your eyes."

"Amber," the Beast said after a pause, "are

you proposing to barber me?"

A flush ran through my whole body. I said, "I suppose you could ask the servants," stiffly.

The Beast ducked his head, making his bulk as small as it could be compared to mine, and leaned forward toward my hand, like a dog seeking forgiveness before he seemed to remember himself and pulled back again. His voice, though, was low and remarkably apologetic. "I would be honored if you were inclined to do so."

"Very well," I said, wondering what I'd gotten myself into, "let's go see if we can make you presentable."

A downright genteel barbering area awaited us in the sitting room beyond the foyer. A copper bath large enough for me to swim in and filled with steaming water sat in front of the fire, with bath sheets big enough for most beds hanging nearby to gather the fire's warmth as well. The Beast's usual chair, which was of preposterous size and allowed him to curl up in a variety of cat-like positions, had been replaced by a proper tilting barber's chair, which made me laugh. "Can you even sit in that?"

"I believe so," the Beast said dubiously. "Whether I want to or not is another question entirely. And then there is the bath."

I regarded the bath, which had to weigh two or three hundred pounds empty. "Do you suppose invisibility lends unexpected strength and efficiency to the serving class?" I expected, and got, no answer, but the comment avoided the topic of the Beast bathing in my presence. He was a Beast; it should not, in any meaningful way, matter. But he was also, it seemed, a prince, and he was certainly a thinking being either way, and also male. I was not unfamiliar with either male anatomy or — the phrase that leapt to mind made me wince — animal husbandry, but somehow the entire activity seemed fraught. "Perhaps there could be bubbles."

"Bubbles," the Beast echoed so swiftly that I thought I wasn't the only one finding the situation questionable, and shortly thereafter I politely turned my back while the Beast settled into a tub full of bubbles.

I turned around again when he gave an unusually human-like groan, and found him jaw-deep in the foam, with his mane floating around him like spiderwebs. "I'd forgotten what a hot bath felt like. I don't usually bathe," he said. "Beasts…don't."

"No, I suppose not." He didn't, as I'd half supposed he would, smell of wet dog. His usual muskiness was strengthened, but not unpleasantly so. I smiled suddenly. "You soak there for a few minutes. I'll be right back."

He gave an agreeable grunt and sank a little

farther into the bubbles. I hurried off to my room, there to test the khemet perfume on my wrist and to think of its spicy warmth melding with the Beast's scent. Yes: I thought it would do nicely. Pleased with myself, I returned to the sitting room, where the Beast was now little more than a blunt face ringed by bubbles, and on impulse put my fingers in the water to touch his mane. His eyes opened, meeting mine, and I asked, "Will I wash it for you?"

I believed that for a moment he actually stopped breathing, though it was hard to tell with the bubbles. Then he nodded, and sat up with a minimum of spillage. I found lightly scented soap and worked it to a lather before sinking my hands into the warmth of his mane. A quick laugh caught me off-guard and shattered my self-consciousness. "And here I'd thought my sisters had a lot of hair."

The Beast breathed laughter, but said nothing. His skull was huge and heavy under my fingertips, like a mastiff's, and the sheer mass of fur meant it took a long time to massage soap through it. The water never got as dirty or as cold as I thought it should. Nor did the bubbles fade, which I found both considerate and vaguely annoying. I was certainly not *peeking*, but neither could I deny a certain prurient interest that slowly intensified as I washed and rinsed and combed his mane with my fingers. My mouth was dry and my cheeks hot as I went through the ritual again, working my way from his scalp through to the ends. Coarse strands clung to my fingers and floated in the water until I captured them into a snarl and set them aside. A jug of warm lemon water appeared at my elbow and rinsed his mane with it, working it through to remove the last of the soap. When I was finally done, I set the jug aside and lowered my mouth to beside his ear, where I murmured, "Are you *purring*, Beast?"

His breath caught, putting a hitch in the purr, and I straightened with a smile. "You *were* purring. I didn't know you could."

"I don't often have reason to." His voice, for a Beast's, was very soft, as if the edges had been taken away by the purr. He shifted, but before he decided to rise, I cried, "Oh, wait! I forgot!" and withdrew the khemet perfume from my bodice to tap a little onto his own wet wrist. He cast me a curious glance, and though I doubted he needed to to catch the scent, lifted his wrist to his nose to inhale.

"You make perfumes?"

"I'm surprised you don't smell my room from half the palace away. Do you—do you like it? It's an ancient recipe, one I found in the library, and I thought—I thought of it, and you, tonight. I thought...I thought of you."

The Beast, smiling as best he was able, took the vial and pressed the perfume's liquid over his palms before raking his huge hands through his mane, scenting it with my perfume. Then he lowered his hands into the water, washing away the excess scent as I, half trying not to be seen, ducked my head to catch the mixture of his scent and the khemet's. It worked even better than I'd imagined, deep and rich and delicious, and I was dizzy when he turned his dreadful smile toward me.

I looked away while he stood, then shrieked with laughter as he shook himself just as any animal would do, spraying water everywhere. I turned with an accusing smile to find as guilty a look as his face could produce writ large across his features, and a bath towel draped around him like a toga. "Well, go on." I turned away again, still smiling, and a few minutes later he cleared his throat, suggesting a reasonable level of decency had been achieved.

A modest amount, at least: he wore trousers and nothing more, as he'd done the first time I'd seen him. Then, though, he had been full of lashing anger, streamlined and dangerous, and now he was distinctly...fuzzy. His mane, though clean, was a tangle from having been shaken, and toweling had rendered the heavy fur on his shoulders and chest fluffy, without enough time having passed for it to lie down again. I went around the tub to run my hands over his shoulders, smoothing the fur, and he lifted his great paws to just barely capture my wrists as he gazed down at me.

My heart lurched so hard spots danced in

front of my eyes and desire stung all the way through me. The Beast was not, perhaps, human, but he was very male, and very close, and wearing the scent I had made for him. Confused, I took a short breath and stepped back. He let me go with such grace that he might not have been holding me at all.

He seemed more like a man to me, somehow, than he had before, although I couldn't convince myself that his form had in any way changed. I whispered, "I should comb your mane before it dries," and he gave the most acquiescent of nods before going to the barber's chair.

My hands, cold with barely acknowledged anticipation, trembled for a long time as I worked a comb through the thick fur. More of it came away, creating shaggy tangles on the floor, and when I noticed a pair of scissors that hadn't been there earlier, I trimmed the ends until they were no longer split and raw. A leather tie came to hand just as I thought I might want one, and I combed his mane back to tie the upper bulk of it in a tail that revealed those unexpectedly elegant ears. All that was left were the eyebrows, which I couldn't reach without tilting the chair back so he would lie beneath me. I worked out how to—a handled gear did the trick—and cautiously tipped the Beast back toward me. He looked up at me a little cross-eyed, murmuring, "I confess I find the idea of scissors near my eyes slightly alarming."

"So do I. I'll be careful." I couldn't, though: my hands shook too much each time I came near his over-growing brows, and I finally tucked the scissors into my bodice and breathed deeply. "I can't. I can't do it upside-down. I'm not sure enough of myself."

"You could," the Beast began in a tone that suggested he was about to say something amusing. He stopped so quickly, though, and looked so distressed, that I was all too easily able to follow his thought, and why the humor in it had gone suddenly flat.

Without giving myself time to think, I said, "I could," and came around the chair to climb onto it, too. To climb onto the Beast, though once I set myself in motion it was less a climb than a lift: he caught me with one tremendous hand and scooped me into the chair with him as if I weighed as little as a pillow. Heat flushed through me, coloring my cheeks and speeding my heartbeat until I could hardly breathe, and even so, I couldn't help but be aware that our shared thought had been predicated on the Beast being a man.

He was not. Had I been lifted so easily into a man's lap, I would have been in his *lap*, even if the nominal goal was to trim his eyebrows. The Beast was too much larger than I for that, and to make things more difficult, he was lying back thanks to the barber's chair. In order to put our faces near to one another, I ended up more across the sharp angle of his ribs than his hips. I doubted my weight bothered him at all, but I felt uncomfortable and absurd.

He dropped his hand and released the chair's catch, sitting up to let the chair move beneath him, and then I *was* in his lap, with his warmth and bulk and the spicy depth of his scent surrounding me. He had a beast's ability to smell. I was quite certain of what my own scent told him, and wondered if my too-fast heartbeat gave me away as well. I felt wild, as if madness had overtaken me, and as if I had no wish to be brought back to sanity.

His mouth was not made for kissing. Nothing either of us could do would change that, but our foreheads touched and I closed my eyes, listening to the tandem harshness of our breath and searching for just a little more bravery. He whispered, "Amber," precursor to a familiar question.

Somehow it gave me the courage I sought. I whispered, "Beast," in return, swiftly curving in on myself to find his jaw, so I could kiss *that*, at least.

The scissors I'd put in my bodice jabbed my belly, and I flinched back from the Beast with a bellowed, "*Ow*! Stars and stones and by the dying mother sun, *fuck*, that hurt!"

The poor Beast elevated from the chair, setting me on my feet and backing away with the haste of a creature who thought he'd damaged me. I withdrew the bloodied scissors, still cursing, and pulled my bodice out so I could see how badly I'd hurt myself. Badly enough: blood oozed from a hole beneath my breastbone, and I pushed the bodice against it again, both to staunch the small wound and for the pain-easing relief of pressure. By then the Beast had retreated halfway across the room, and I snarled—unfairly, but pain brought out the worst in me— "It wasn't you. I put the sun-blasted scissors in my bodice so I could trim your eyebrows and then forgot they were there. I jabbed myself."

Halfway through the explanation its absurdity began to strike me, and although it still hurt like the moon's broken heart, I concluded with a reluctant laugh. "I'm sorry. I didn't mean to yell at you. It wasn't your fault."

The Beast passed a hand over his eyes in the most human gesture I'd seen from him yet, then threw the motion away. "The servants had better take a look, then. Clean it, heal it if they can. I'll leave you to it."

"Beast," I said in a smaller voice, as he left the room, "will you—will you be at dinner?" It wasn't the question I meant to ask, but I lacked the boldness for the other, though only a minute earlier, the other's answer had been at hand.

He stopped at the door, looking at me. Studying me, as if he'd heard the question I hadn't asked, the one *he* asked every night, before shaking his great head once. "No, I don't think so. Not tonight. Good night, Amber."

I waited until he was gone, then let out a bereft little laugh, and let the servants tend to my injury.

They gave me a potion so potent I didn't care that they also gave me two stitches, or that each breath stung a little. I kept my eyes closed through all of it, conscious that I believed, rightly or wrongly, that it was easier for the invisible staff to do their jobs if I wasn't trying to watch them do it. Their humming and fussing seemed less muted than usual, as if the drink had rendered me closer to their state. I found the consequent higher pitch of their buzzing disturbing, even upsetting, and as soon as they seemed done with me, fled the parlor-cum-bathing-room.

In my altered state, I was not at all surprised that I could not find my rooms. I marched down the hallway, occasionally bumping off the walls and equally often picking myself up from the floor, and waited for the enchantment to take advantage of my muddled head. Even expecting it, I still didn't quite notice when the visions began, perhaps because they entwined nicely with my half-acknowledged fantasies of the Beast. They faded together, blood-heating images of my great Beast with my knees over his shoulders and his tongue between my thighs, and equally aching visions of my hands knotted in a dark-skinned woman's hair, urging *her* tongue to carry me to ecstasy. She crawled up my body, burying her fingers within me, a thing even fevered imagination admitted the Beast and his claws could not do, and lingered at my breasts until I cried with need and pleasure. She covered her mouth with mine as I broke for her, and she whispered, "How could I go on without you, my Nell?" as I shuddered and gasped and sank back into the sheets.

"You would find a new king," I murmured, when I could speak again. "A new man to pleasure you in bed, while I stood by and went mad with jealousy."

"Never."

"But you would." I rolled my queen onto her belly, stroking her thighs until they began to part. "You miss a man's touch. You still say his name at night, sometimes."

"Your touch is all I want right now." The queen's voice was ragged, and grew more so as I teased promises from her in the pursuit of satisfaction. Then, because I could, I refused to finish her until she had brought me to a head again, and her desperation to please made my release all the sweeter.

She went away often, did my queen, and I could never quite forgive her for it, no matter how important the treaty, no matter how necessary the war. I would dress her in her armor and leave her wanting, so she would remember to come back to me, and I recalled her sensual, shameful flush when her desire was so great that mounting her horse cascaded her into release. I teased her mercilessly when she returned from that campaign, urging her to admit to the thrill she'd felt with a beast between her legs. "No one," she promised me, "no one could ever love a beast as I love you."

While she campaigned and I sated myself with her love, the prince grew from a child to a youth, always standing at my side as his mother rode away. "Why does she always go?"

I put my arm around his shoulder, kissed his hair, and replied, "Because she doesn't love you like I do, my sweet." He turned a gaze on me that would have broken his mother's heart, but I was not his mother, and never had been.

Time passed: Irindala came and went, her son growing in leaps and fits from a youth to a young man. He had his mother's look about him: large dark eyes and curling black hair, and in time, I saw all that I desired about her reflected in him. He charmed and flirted, delighting the ladies of the court, and though I taught him to dance and seduce with his gaze, he never turned that sweet look on me. A worm of envy began to grow in my breast, that others should have what I did not. Irindala returned home and to my bed, and for a little while I was satisfied, until late one night, our limbs tangled together, light and dark, she murmured to me that she would bring her son with her on her next campaign, so he could begin to learn politics in the real world, and not just from books.

My heart cracked, not with fear, but with anger. "Are you sure he'll want to go?"

"It's his duty."

"And you'll leave me here, alone, with neither of you?"

"Who better to watch over my kingdom while we're gone?" She put herself above me and showered me with kisses, but even her hunger to satisfy me could not thaw my anger. I would not be abandoned by both for the sake of politics; the son could be sent to try his uncertain hand, or Irindala could go alone, but I would not lose them both. They belonged to me, Irindala because she loved me and the boy because I had raised him for her sake. I would have no other answer but that one of them would stay and be mine. But Irindala was accustomed to leaving, and I knew I could never keep her. The boy, then, would stay, no matter what enchantment I had to work to make it so.

I had done no magic since giving Irindala the boundary spell that she had worked with her husband's bones and her own blood. I had not needed to: she had been willingly seduced, and the power of being the queen's lover and confidante was stronger in human courts than almost any faery magic could ever be. We were creatures of magic, shaped in form by our desires, and the longer we went without using our power, the stronger it became, distilled in our blood. The boy did not see me with a lover's eyes, and so I made myself into a thing that he would: sweet and bosomy, with hair like his mother's, and a boldness that would run suddenly dry and require coaxing to be brought again to the fore. I let him seduce me, leaving him never knowing that it was I who seduced him.

I came to the court by day a precious creature lost in wonderment, even foregoing the roses I so often embroidered into my clothes, so that I might not be measured against my other self, Irindala's lover. By night I went to Irindala's bed, more passionate than ever from the pursuit of her son. The same touches that brought cries from her throat elicited shudders in the youth: teasing lips plucking nipples, curved nails scraping sensitive centers. No faery was ever more sated by love and desire than I, but rage clouded my joy whenever the queen mentioned her next journey, and her intention of taking her son with her. "The courtiers say he has a mistress, my queen. Perhaps he won't want to leave her."

She laughed beneath my warning, and gasped as I took her more ferociously. Only after, her lips against my breast, did she murmur, "I've heard the rumor, but I've not seen the girl, so perhaps she doesn't exist. He'll still come, Nell. It remains his duty."

I rose from the bed cold and angry, determined to win protestations of love and promises of forever from the boy I had raised to manhood. I shed the form that Irindala loved as I walked to his rooms, replacing it with the curves and large eyes that had captured his heart, and I was welcomed into his bed by eager hands. My anger could not quite hold as I admired the beauty of his face, and in holding my breasts to his tongue, I knew I could win from him the promises I desired.

And then came a thing I did not expect: Irindala at his door, Irindala who had followed me, Irindala who saw through my enchantment, and cried, "Nell!" in horror as I rode above the lad and let his fingers work between my legs.

The saying of my name shattered the magic holding me in my young lover's preferred form. His face contorted in abhorrence as I became the minder he had known all his life. He cast me off him with the strength of disgust, and seized a blanket as he came to his feet, covering himself from my gaze. "Aunt Nell, what—what have you done to me?"

I spat, "Nothing you weren't eager for," but he shook his head, dark eyes large and horrified.

"No. No, I wanted my little Helen, not—" A

shudder ran through him. "What a fool I am. Nell. You might have called yourself Cornelia, too, or Ellen, and I never would have thought. Mother, Mother, I—I didn't know, I didn't want—!"

"You are *never* to blame," Queen Irindala said. For the first time I saw her *as* a queen, as a great and terrible warrior, and I knew that in a handful of heartbeats, her wrath would fall upon me.

"Traitor!" I shrieked at her son, knowing him to be the weaker of the two. "I raised you, I loved you, you desired me—"

"No more than I desired a beast!"

A wicked laugh shot from my throat. I pointed at both of them, Queen and Prince alike, and whispered, "Oh, but your mother knows love for a beast, do you not, Irindala? I curse you," I spat. "I curse the blood that runs in your veins, child, that it shall never let you die. I curse the body that you live in, that it should be as a beast's. I curse the walls that you call home, that they should forever be an unsolvable maze. I curse those who serve you that they should be as unseen as they are unappreciated. I curse the very land that you walk upon that it should be as if salted."

A maelstrom rose, the prince's cries at its heart. All the beasts of the forest and plains fought to become a part of him, his bones breaking and stretching, fur erupting from his skin as he screamed. Power flowed from me, ripping away the vestiges of humanity I had so long worn and revealing the immortal, ethereal beauty that was my own, for in no other form could I convey deathlessness upon a mortal creature. I shrieked in outraged pleasure, then, through the howl and the wind, through the shattering of stone and the falling of walls, heard Irindala whisper, "This land is *mine*," and I knew I had made a mistake.

I had given her the spell myself, told her how to waken it, how to bind the borders of the land against her enemies. She had bled for it, buried bones for it, spoken prayers over it, and made it her own. It was a spell to last forever, holding the borders of her country so long as the blood of the queen who laid it ran true in the veins of its royal family.

But as much as it bound the land to her, it bound Irindala to the land as well, and not even the faery queen herself could contain all the power of the earth within her mighty grasp.

"You can't!" I cried. "*You cannot*! The borders will weaken, your reign will end! You cannot, Irindala! It loses you all you have fought for!"

"It gains me my son." Soft, implacable words, and with them she tore from me the darkest aspects of my curse: that immortality should only last so long as the beastly form, and that the form itself could be undone by a lover's willing touch. That the maze of his home should become an endless palace, the servants offer what solace they could, and the land barren but for gardens of roses.

We fought, myself with the power borne within me, and Irindala with the power of the land. Forest grew around us, and a palace rose, and all the while the prince roared and sobbed and struggled with his transformation. I seized the roses, making them mine: should any traveler seeking shelter enter this sanctuary, they might leave safely unless they plucked a rose. Irindala poured strength into the forest, extending it as her beastly son's demesne; I took away his freedom to roam it, but could not prevent her making him its protector, and the protector of all the beasts within. I stole his rationality; she returned a thread, which grasped, might lead him back to thoughtfulness. On and on we went, until she cast the last and greatest counter to my spell: the land itself rejected me, casting me beyond the borders into my own land, and her voice lingering in my ears promised me that I should never return unless love itself carried me past the bone-bred barriers.

I howled protest, digging my hands into earth I had not set foot on in a hundred years or more, and wept as a rising spring showed me a face that was my own.

I opened my eyes with a head on me like a

drum, and for some time lay where I was, with no idea and not much interest in where that might be. Only my head hurt. It seemed like my belly ought to, where I'd stabbed it, but when I flexed the muscles there, I felt no protest of pain, or even bandages. Looking hardly seemed worth it. Not when I could see, as if at the backs of my eyes, the vision I had been left with.

I'd known the eyes, the quirk of the lips, the unevenness that made it compelling. I had not known the highness of the cheekbones or the slight length of jaw; those things belonged to Pearl, not me. Neither had I known the ears, long and slender and pointed, not unlike the Beast's. But the face, yes. I had known that face, because it was my own.

I tried to sit up with the grim intention of finding the Beast, and discovered two things: one, sitting up was all but beyond me, and two, the Beast sat beside me as if he had not moved for hours. He was reading, in fact. He wore a carefully constructed set of spectacles, and was reading aloud, though I had hardly heard him in the midst of my own thoughts. I recalled the last words he'd said with a hazy memory: something of morning and evening mists, and now, as he made to close the book, I said, "I'm afraid you'll have to start again. I seem to have missed most of the story."

"Amber!" He cast the book aside and caught one of my hands in both of his enormous paws, engulfing half my arm in the effort. "Amber, thank the stars."

"I'm having a hard time moving. I feel like I've been sleeping for a week."

"Not a week." His voice lowered, vibrating through me. "Ten days days, Amber."

"Ten days." I understood him, but in the same way I had when he had first captured me and told me I had to stay: I understood the content of the words without them meaning much. Then, as his worried expression made it clear I must have, indeed, been asleep a very long time, I said, "I suppose I must be very hungry, then. And that I need very badly to pee."

Both of those things, having been considered, became violently true. I still all but lacked the strength to stand, but the Beast whisked me from the bed with the grace of practice, and deposited me over a chamber pot. I squatted there for some time, too relieved both literally and figuratively to be humiliated, and simply said, "Help," when my bladder had emptied and I couldn't yet push myself up. The Beast lifted me again, his head close to mine as he rumbled, "The bed or a chair?"

My eyes closed as I inhaled his scent. "You're still wearing my perfume."

"I hoped it would comfort you." He sounded pleased that I'd noticed, and I clung to his shoulders a few moments before sighing, "A chair, I think."

Only when he carried me into the sitting room did I realize we weren't in my rooms at all: there were no perfume potions anywhere, and the decorating was in different colors. My confusion showed, because the Beast said, "These are my rooms. I found you outside my door, the morning after my bath," as he tucked me into a chair.

If that polite description was how we were to refer to that evening, I would gladly accept it. "And I've slept all that time? I was... dreaming. *Not* dreaming."

"I told you the enchantment might try to kill you, if it couldn't make you fit into its story. I brought a few things from your rooms. Your rose water, and your amber mirror." The Beast fetched a platter that had appeared while he tucked me in. It was my usual breakfast, with a pile of bacon taller than my hand, and with my hand mirrorr and a vial of the rose water placed neatly on its side.

I touched the mirror's back, but didn't pick it up. "I doubt I want to look at myself." Nor did I wish to conjure up images of my family, not right now. Instead I offered the Beast some bacon. Somewhat to my surprise, he accepted. For a while we sat together and ate, before I finally pushed the plate away. "I'm not sure it was trying to kill me. Beast, my mother's name was Eleanor."

I had never seen him swallow before, not

the way a human did when they were startled or afraid. A long, cautious silence passed, before he said, "My mother banished her."

"My father fought in the Border Wars."

The Beast came to his feet in a swift motion, knocking his chair backward. He caught it with one quick hand, settling it before stalking the outskirts of the room as if it had suddenly become a cage. Nervousness twisted my stomach, but not the fear I'd once had of him. When he reached the window, he asked, "Do you know what caused them?"

"The Border Wars? No. I mean — no. I know the queen..." I knew a great deal more about the queen now than I had the last time I'd been awake, and spent a moment determining what I *had* known. "Everyone knows she fought off invaders after the king died, and that the borders were safe for decades after that. But forty years ago they began to weaken again, and by thirty years ago they had to be re-established in the Border Wars. I know they say some of our enemies weren't human, that they were faeries, but I never used to believe that. There are hardly even any witches, how could there be faeries? But now I know that there were faeries. Beast...I have to leave. I have to go talk to my father. I need to know... what he knew about my mother."

"I need to show you something." It wasn't a refusal, though in truth, at this stage I didn't expect to be refused. Too much had happened, here and between us. I put my hand out, and he returned to not only take it, but once more scooped me gently into his arms. He brought me to his balcony, and I saw immediately what he wanted me to.

Roses had run amok, in the days that I slept. They were no longer fighting the forest at the estate's perimeter: instead they swept toward the palace like a pernicious weed. The long drive and the beautifully maintained ponds were blanketed in greenery; if that greenery hadn't been spotted with color I would have thought it to be greedy, grasping ivy. It covered the ground in the same way, layering tendrils that stuck to the earth and cement and stone. Ivy, especially new ivy, could be torn up relatively easily, but I knew from experience that the rose vines were protected by vicious thorns.

I caught motion from the corner of my eye, but it stopped when I looked directly. I glanced away again, watching side-eyed, and saw pieces of encroaching roses being scraped away from the palace walls in swaths, like someone was running the edge of a spade along the building and loosening them. No one was there, or at least, no one visible: the servants fought to keep the palace safe in whatever way that they could.

Their handiwork had not, though, been able to disguise the roses' trajectory. They were growing purposefully, coming from all directions, and from the shrinking circle where they had not yet reached, it was clear that their destination was where the Beast stood with me safe in his arms.

"They've been coming for me since you fainted," he said softly, but I shook my head.

"They're Nell's roses, Beast. They're not coming for you. They want me to finish her story."

"No." The Beast released me when I made to squirm away, but his deep voice reverberated despair as he did so. "Amber, no. You said yourself that the roses didn't like you."

"That was before they knew who I was. Before *I* knew who I was." I took a shaking step to the balcony's rail, leaning on it. I extended my hand, and we could both see the leading vines grow, adding six inches as they tried to reach me. I closed my fingers again and they faltered. "You see," I said quietly. "I'm sorry. She found a way to get to you. I'm the villain, Beast."

He growled, "Really," but I knew the growl wasn't for me. "Did you deliberately lose your family's fortune? Set fire to your home? Plan to force eight people to a remote hunting lodge? Conjure a snowstorm so you were driven to my palace? Then you are not the villain." He closed a massive paw on the balcony rail. "At worst, you're a pawn, like myself, Amber. A victim of someone else's game."

"But she was my mother."

"She was all but mine as well, and more." The Beast shuddered, and I forgot the threat approaching us to put my hand over his.

"I'm sorry, Beast. For what she did to you. That was wrong."

"I should have known."

A little smile crept across my face. "Now, you can't have it both ways, Beast. Either we're both innocent of being victim of her manipulations, or neither of us are, and you seem determined that I am."

He looked down at me a long moment, then turned his hand under mine, clasping it. "Very well. I have...a great deal of unlearning to do, if that's how it's to be. I've blamed myself for —"

"A very long time. Over a century, and yet Irindala still reigns beyond this forest. How?"

"Enchantment." A brief smile curled his mouth at my exasperated look. "Beyond that I don't know. I was not...thoughtful...in the aftermath of Eleanor's curse. The magic has told me time and again how I was brought here, but it can't finish the story. It can only try to make the pieces it has fit the story it knows so far, and it doesn't seem to know what happened after the curse struck."

"Which is why I must go to Father. He must know something. He knows my mother — and

Maman, for that matter — both knew the queen, once upon a time. He must know something more."

The Beast looked askance at me. "Both his wives knew my mother? Your father moves in high circles, Amber."

"He used to. You can come with me, can't you?" I asked, suddenly eager. "You protect this forest and its beasts, don't you? So you must be able to leave the palace grounds."

"No longer. It is your world, a world apart from mine. I used to be able to." The Beast reached toward the roses, which surged toward him with thorns sharp and wicked at the fore. He pulled his hand back again and the vines settled. "It's been like this since they began their attack. I think they cannot kill me, but I believe they can bind me. Keep me here. And that they *will* kill me, if they can. Which is another reason I don't believe you're the villain, Amber. The roses have always fought the forest, never coming for me. Now they've turned their focus inward, and — can you walk?" he asked. "You should see this from the observatory."

"I think I can. Wait." I collected my mirror and the rose water, though the mirror seemed more likely to be useful. We might be able to see beyond the forest with it, or find a way through the roses with it. The rose water went into my bodice, but I had to find a reticule for the mirror, and tied the purse at my hip before we left the Beast's rooms. I meant to ask him *why* he had brought the mirror, but between my weariness and the obvious answer—that he knew its properties, and always had—I couldn't muster the effort. Even without wasting energy speaking, I tired halfway to the observatory. The Beast unhesitatingly carried me to its narrow stairway, which I had to ascend myself; his bulk was too great for him to climb the stairs carrying anything. He stayed just behind me, in case I fainted, but we reached the glass dome in safety, and I saw at once what he meant.

It wasn't only the roses racing toward the house. The lands had shrunk beneath the forest's encroachment as well. In places it was clear a war was being waged: swiftly-growing saplings were being throttled by roses, but their branches bent to scrape the vines from the ground. Here and there they'd reached a stalemate, horrible tangles of roses and trees no longer trying to reach the house, but instead growing higher and higher, each trying to dominate the other. "All this in ten days?"

"The snarls are from when I ventured out. It seemed to help: the roses stopped where I was, and the forest was able to catch up, to hold them in place. But staying still in their midst that long..." The Beast exhaled. "As I said, I think they can't kill me, but they could bind me. And I was afraid what would happen to you, if I let them take me. So I came back." He was silent a little while before saying, "I am not certain whether I am a coward or not."

"Beast! No! Of course not. If the roses did take you, she'd have won, wouldn't she? And if she won, the palace would go to ruin and I would die too. It's not cowardice to leave a battle you can't win, not if retreating saves lives. Even one life." I considered that. "I suspect I may feel especially strongly about the matter when it's *my* life."

That earned a chuckle from the Beast, which was all I wanted. "I have to go see Father," I said again. "If it was the full moon I could wait on Pearl conjuring a mirror-spell again—"

The Beast, cautiously, said, "Have you learned anything of *your* mirror?"

"I have. Oh!" I pressed my palm against the mirror's purse, then sank onto one of the low cushioned seats, putting my face in my hands. "Of course. That's why it worked for me, isn't it? We're all Eleanor's daughters. Of course Pearl's witchery didn't awaken out of nowhere. I knew—I knew, once you said the stones were bespelled, that the pearl was magic, that you hoped she would learn to use it and be able to break the enchantment here. If I go to Father I can bring her back, Beast. She can help you. She can fight the curse from within."

"She cannot." The Beast's voice was strange, and I looked up at him with fingers pressed against my mouth. "The breaking of the enchantment is quite specific, and I cannot imagine Pearl succumbing to its requirements in any usefully timely fashion."

"But she's a witch," I said helplessly. "I don't understand." And then I did, Irindala's amelioration of the curse coming back to me: *the form could be undone by a lover's willing touch.* I stood, swiftly, and the Beast, with a desperate ache in his voice, asked, "Amber, will you sleep with me?"

I opened my mouth to cry *yes!*, and rose vines smashed through the observatory windows to snatch me away.

Thorns sank into my skin as the roses held me, kept me from writhing away. Within a heartbeat I didn't dare struggle, as the runners reared back from the palace and fell toward the ground. Roses, even enchanted roses, weren't meant to hold a human's weight four or five stories above the earth, and all that kept me from plummeting were the numbers of runners rising to catch me. I felt them weaken and buckle beneath me, and others take up their slack. Those that pulled away left scores in my dress and across my limbs, though the pain wasn't as great as I would have imagined. It stung and tingled, but the roses I'd picked had caused me more discomfort.

I glimpsed the Beast leaping through the broken observatory windows and pouncing after the runners, his claws glittering sharp and his roar so loud and endless I briefly mistook it for the wind. He skidded to a halt at the roof's edge, slate tiles shattering and flying free beneath his weight, but I was already out of reach. Screaming, reaching for him, but out of reach. A runner wrapped around my face and lodged in my mouth, muffling my screams. I bit it, trying to catch a breath to scream again, and felt leaves tickling the back of my throat. I bit down again, tasting bitter sap, and a story exploded inside my mind.

@}-,-`-. ~ .-`-,-{@

I was Eleanor, and I never left the borders to Irindala's country, always testing them with my thwarted rage. They could not hold: Irindala had spent too much magic in altering my curse. I knew it, and yet they held. For years I paced, hatred sustaining me, and then it came to me that an active enemy lent strength to any magic. I gathered power into myself, transforming until my roots ran deep and my blooms rose to the sun: a hedge of roses that crept along the border, adding beauty as it searched for weakness. I grew tenaciously enough that in time the area I patrolled became known as the Rose Border, and it was at the Rose Border that the Border Wars both ended and began.

She ought not have lived that long, my old lover the queen. No mortal could, and no spell, no matter how flawlessly wrought, could forever survive the price of a single person maintaining it. Its burden had been meant to pass from queen to child, its strength invigorated by new blood. It took decades longer than I expected, but one day my wandering tendrils pressed into the border, and the border gave.

I plucked and picked, weakening it, though the banishment held: I couldn't cross the border myself. When I was sure of its weakening, I gathered myself together again, reshaping my form to the faery I had once been, and went into the Border Kingdom with news that the human border had finally begun to fail.

It could hardly be thought of as an *invasion*. Fae whose memories were long and whose pride stung at having been pushed back by a human army merely went to see for themselves, and, where they could, edged into Irindala's country. Elsewhere, where the border fell between Irindala's country and other human realms, there *were* invasions. Irindala's people had lived in undisturbed peace for seventy years or more, under the guidance of a queen believed to be a witch; invasion was inevitable. Having spread my knowledge, I returned to the border to sit and shiver with delight at each new piece of gossip about the slow fall of Irindala's country.

She fought for seven years, an ancient unaging queen struggling to retain her country, and in the seventh year, in a lull, retired from the field. That, finally, was when the faery king attacked, pushing hisy kingdom forward like an arrow meant to pierce the heart of Irindala's country. I thrilled to it, feeling my banishment weaken as the king advanced: I could not be kept from a conquered country whose land no longer belonged to its former queen. I thought her too old, too defeated by the long-ago loss of her son, to rally, and yet somehow, I was wrong.

Irindala returned to the battle as an implacable shield to her people. Everywhere she went, the border strengthened again, strengthened as it had not done in the previous seven years of war. Strengthened as though the aged queen re-cast the spell I had taught her nearly a century ago, though to do so was impossible. It required royal blood and royal bones, and unless she plucked the very bones from her own body, I could not see how she managed, for she had never again married, and had sworn for all this time to hold the land for the prince's return.

I entertained the glorious idea that she had sacrificed *him*, her beastly child, but I would have known that in my own bones, and knew it to be untrue. I had never tested the spell I'd given her, though, and thought that perhaps after all this time, her own blood renewed the magic after all. It did not much matter, perhaps; what mattered was that she pushed the Border Kingdom back, and back again, until the bloodiest battle of the war was fought at the Rose Border, and I, architect of it all, nearly died beneath a mortal's steel blade.

It was not that I was a female that stopped him; there were women a-plenty amongst Irindala's army, and the blood on his blade said he'd killed without hesitation before. Nor was it that I was not obviously a combatant: innumerable of the fair folk went into battle with no visible armor, relying on their magic to protect them more thoroughly than metal ever could. No: it was something else, a sudden focus in his gaze, and then a far-away look that ended with his sword lowering, and his deep voice saying, "Go."

I rose, and ran, and that night reshaped myself, for the first time in decades, to a mortal form. I kept those aspects of myself that I was most fond of: the slight asymmetry of my face, my height and my bosom, but I squared my jaw and cast off the white fairness of my hair for a honey gold, making of myself a creature that Irindala would not recognize if she met me face to face —

— though, remembering that she had known me in my sweet Helen form, I thought it best that I never encounter the queen again. Nor did I need to; all I needed was to find the man who had not slain me. And so I did, by putting myself to work in the roving hospital the queen's army had set up on the faery kingdom's side of the border. I listened and watched and waited, and soon enough he came in with an injury he said was no more than a scratch. He smiled at me as if I might be someone familiar as I tended the wound, and ten weeks later when Irindala closed the border for the second time in her long life, I returned to her country as Jacob's bride.

I finally knew, when Jacob carried me across the border into the country I had been banished from, *how* Irindala had survived a century and more. I put my feet into the soil, and felt how the earth, while fit for crops and building, had no *magic* in it. All life had magic, and we faeries, more than that, but Irindala's country had been drained of its power. The only place I felt any at all was along the re-established border, and that was new magic, fresh, recently cast. It had not yet spread into the land, and I thought it never would, not with Irindala drawing on the land to sustain her life. Here and there the earth was even spoiled, barren with too much having been taken from it. A thrill shivered through me. Irindala might well be her own undoing, and never know what horrors she had wrought. But that was only probable, and I intended her downfall to be inevitable.

I had no excuse to ask my new husband whether witches abounded here, but it took little enough time to confirm what I suspected. Witches were almost as unheard of as faeries, and even those who fought in the Border Wars only half believed in the fair folk at all. I dared not draw attention to myself as a witch, then, though I had been known as one while at Irindala's side. I did what I could, growing lush roses along the walls of the merchant's mansion Jacob earned his way to owning, and when he shook his head at them, I laughed and said, "Our own rose border, my love. Did the last one not bring us together?" We seduced one another amongst the roses, in the heart of my power, and I, forgetting caution in my hunger for a long-absent touch, became careless, and thus round with our passion.

Jacob's reverence at my swollen belly surpassed any love or awe Irindala had ever held me in, and I loved him for it. A daughter we called Pearl was born, and when it became clear to me that her hair would come in as white as my own naturally did, I worked the smallest enchantment on her, that it should be strikingly sable: worthy of attention, but not accusations of witchery. I set it to last so long as she wished to confine herself to the expected and the ordinary, which was as close to forever as any spell could be set, and was satisfied to see her grow up a cool and quick child who judged with a scathing glance.

Time and again I returned to lie in the roses with Jacob, and from those unions came the second daughter, Opal, who even at birth was so mild and ordinary that I lost interest in her immediately, and in due time, the third, Amber, whose golden gaze earned her the name and upon whom I cast a spell like Pearl's, softening the gold with green so she should not be thought a witch even in childhood. Unlike with Pearl, the spell seemed to reduce her fire and ambition, but she was the only one of the girls who loved the roses as much as I did, and so I was fond of her despite her dullness.

Irindala discovered me when Amber was two.

A queen was not meant to visit her demesne without fanfare; she was not supposed to slip from city to town and village, meeting the people as another, ordinary person. Afterward, I suspected that at some time or another nearly everyone in her kingdom had met their queen, and that almost none of them knew it.

I descended from our carriage outside an acquaintance's home, prepared to do the necessary duty of smiling and praising that seemed useful to Jacob's business. As the footman released my hand, I looked up from watching my footing and gazed directly into Irindala's eyes.

She had changed hardly at all, wearing her decades as a bare handful of years. Her beauty and resolution were undiminished, her carriage proud, and her dress of modern style, a detail I, who still loved the gowns of old, felt a flash of admiration for. I had for years worn a disguise, a face different from the one she had known, but, as she had done before, she saw through the enchantment in an instant, as evidenced by a hatred as potent as the day we had parted.

I had only one weapon at my disposal in that moment, and curtsied low, crying, "My queen!" in ringing tones that could only alert all who heard me of the illustrious presence we were in.

By the time I rose from my curtsy, Irindala was gone, and everyone in earshot looked at me with sympathy-tainted amusement: clearly they believed me to have lost my mind, and I received no small amount of mockery for it upon alighting in my acquaintance's sitting room. No one, it seemed, had seen the woman fitting my description, and I was obliged to concede, in public at least, that I had been taken by some fit of amusing madness.

I did not stay where she might find me. She had weakened my curse and lived a century since, and though *I* knew the cost it might wreak from her country should she gather her power to destroy me, *she* seemed not to, and I never doubted that she would hunt me like a dog and end me in the street, if she could.

I cast the greatest magic I had in years, and left Jacob and his daughters believing that their wife and mother had died giving birth to dull little Amber. Then I fled, not toward the border where she might expect me to run, but deeper into her kingdom, until at the edge of the enchanted forest, I flung myself into the earth and traveled farther, until I could rise as roses around the palace that held Irindala's beastly son.

I came to myself, once more Amber and no longer Nell, retching in the heart of a rose thicket. Sap clung to my throat, clogging my breath, while tears and snot ran from my face as I tried again and again to purge the sap from my body. The roses, which had never had a voice before, cooed *daughter* at me, and I gagged on the word. Petals shivered like laughter and leaves stroked my back, a motherly touch that made sobs break through the sap plugging my throat.

You are, though, the roses said. *Lift your hands, child. See your blood.*

I didn't want to. I couldn't stop myself. My hands rose, thorn pricks and scrapes all over them. The blood was gold and sticky as sap, with flecks of red swirling through like roses in amber. I had enough breath now, and screamed, "*No!*" with such force that I doubled myself, then fell to my knees coughing bloody sap.

He belongs to me, the roses purred. *The bestial prince is yours, and you are mine, so he belongs to me.*

I panted, "No," again, and pushed to my feet, knowing I pushed my hands against thorns and hardly feeling the pain. Nor would I look at the wounds, at the wrongness of my blood, and I feared what the mirror at my hip would show me of my eyes. I turned in the thicket, waiting for Eleanor to appear in a mortal form. Instead the roses gathered together, creating a shape of petals and stems that had some approximation of a human face. She could see me: of that I had no doubt. But why she chose to remain roses lingered in my mind as a mystery for a few heartbeats, before I laughed roughly. "You're stuck, aren't you? You came into the queen's forest and even all your power can't bring you back to your faery form, not at the heart of the enchantment. You're stuck."

Runners lashed out and struck my face, scoring wounds and narrowly missing my eyes. *Stuck, but not helpless. Watch your tongue, daughter.*

"I'm not your daughter." But I was, of course. I was, and that had to give me some kind of weapon to use against her, if only I could think of it. My blood was half hers. More than half, perhaps, I thought, looking at sap rising from my stinging scrapes.

The rose runners had known me, when I'd reached toward them in the palace. They'd reached back. Maybe they knew me still. I turned from Eleanor, not trying to escape her notice, but for the moment's respite from her strangely formed body. It began to shape itself again in front of me, but I whispered, "I want out," and extended both my bloody hands.

Pearl would have been better at it. Pearl had spent months already in the pursuit of witchcraft. All I could do was think I had sap in my veins, as there was sap in the living roses, and ask them to let me pass, as sisters might.

They didn't. Eleanor swirled into being in front of me again, laughter in her rose-petal eyes. Anger rose in me, different from before. That, though voiced as denial, had been born of fear. This was calmer, born of defiance, and felt stronger for it. "What is amber but the resin of healing wounds?"

A flicker of something curled Eleanor's leafy lip, and my own mouth curled with cold anger. This time I reached out not with the hope of moving the roses, but holding them still. The rustling branches protested, then slowed, then held. I couldn't freeze them as solidly as true amber, but I had seen innumerable lumps of half-frozen resin trickling down trees, hard enough to poke and dent without easily regaining their shape, and that was enough. I didn't try to make a passage with magic, only ran into the brambles, trusting that I would survive the scratches and regrow the hair caught and pulled free. I pressed and pushed branches out of my way, careless with my skin, and knew there would be a price paid for every puncture. Where I could, I dropped low, crawling through the thicket, and it was on my hands and knees that I made my escape.

It was not a clearing that I reached, but rather a different kind of tangle: I had reached a border where the forest and the roses fought each other. Here, though, the undergrowth lifted for me, tree roots carving a tunnel of themselves and the forest floor that I could scramble through. The passage collapsed behind me, and for voiceless blooms, the roses screamed quite well, their rage reverberating in my very blood. I cast my thoughts forward, thinking of my magic-born sisters, and of Father, and of what he knew. I followed those thoughts as if they were a lifeline, scrambling ever onward, denying the part of me that was drawn back toward the roses.

Somewhere beyond the distance I knew the palace walls to be, the forest let me surface, and the ground beneath my feet remained curiously clear of roots and lumpy hillocks. I ran, and then I walked, and then I ran some more, not so much choosing a direction as simply running *away*. I had stood above the estate in the observatory, and knew that the hunting lodge was not, by ordinary travel, within a day's journey of the palace. I had little hope of finding my way home, but I remembered the Beast had told me Father would be home before nightfall, and I thought maybe the forest might have enough magic left to guide me.

I had been running—and walking and gasping and limping—for an hour or two when I burst onto a small, wealthy farmstead. A handsome barn stood at one corner of a very large garden; at the corner diagonal rose a whitewashed house whence happily raised voices could be heard. The far side of the house was covered in roses, huge rich flowers that had no business blooming this early in the season, but bloom they did. Land had been cleared beyond another corner, with the foundations of a new building already built, and between that building and the barn lay pens with pigs and goats. The earth hazed with the green of new growth, and it all seemed prosperous and safe.

It wasn't until Beauty plodded out of the barn with Flint in tow that I realized the prettily whitewashed house was the hunting lodge, and the farm, our own. I let go a cry of relief and thanks to the forest, and plunged down toward the oldest of my little brothers, who gaped at me as if I was a ghost appearing from the woods. Then he cried, "Amber! *Amber*!" and before I'd reached him, almost the whole of the family had spilled from the house to meet me. Even Pearl, whom I had not believed *could*, spilled tears as the family captured me in hugs, all of them shouting questions.

Opal finally shushed them by saying, beneath the uproar, "But look at the state of you, Amber," in dismay. I did, and wondered that they'd been willing to approach me at all. My dress, which had only been a sleeping gown to begin with, was in tatters, and thorn scrapes criss-crossed my skin until I appeared hardly more than a walking welt. I touched my hair, hardly able to imagine its condition, and Jasper, with a forthrightness bordering on uninhibited delight, said, "It's *awful!*"

I laughed in surprise and hugged him. "Thank you. I'm sure that made me feel better than an 'it's not so bad'."

"It is so bad," he continued with that same good cheer. "You've got half a rosebush in your hair, Amber." He reached to pluck a thorn from the tangles. I caught his hand with a swiftness that startled both of us, and shook my head. "Don't. Don't touch them. I don't trust them."

"Amber," Pearl said, her voice heavy, "what's happened? Did the Beast do this to you?"

"What? No! Stars, no. No, it's—" I looked at Father, whose eyes were still bright with tears, and whose mouth was a grim anticipatory line in a beard he had not worn the last time I'd seen him. "It wasn't the Beast," I said again, firmly. "Father, I have to know. What did you know of your first wife?"

Father's grimness swept away in a flood of astonishment soon replaced by aged resignation. "Less than I should have. Come, children. We'd better go inside."

Only when we stepped inside did I realize who had been missing from the crowd outdoors. "Maman?" I asked, suddenly frightened. "Where is Maman?"

"Resting upstairs," Opal said quietly. "She took to her bed over a week ago, and has hardly been aware of us since. Amber, what has happened to you?"

A tremor of relief raised hairs on my arms. Maman had always been fragile, all of her strength drained by the boys and the letters she wrote, but the prospect of her loss while I had been away was too much to bear. I wanted to see her, but my story needed to be told, and would only agitate her. Opal could come up with some softer variant on it, something palatable for Maman's infirm state, and we would share that with her, instead of the whole dreadful truth.

We sat together, all of us, even little Jet, whose three years certainly should have protected him from the worst of my tale. Helpless to explain the impossible in anything but blunt terms, I told them what I had learned of the queen, the curse, and Eleanor's role in it.

Pearl went and got a mirror when I spoke of the spell that had altered her hair, staring into it as if trying to understand that the brilliant white coif she now wore was what she had always been meant to have. Then she handed *me* the mirror, and my story fell into speechlessness as I gazed at it.

The green was gone from my eyes, leaving them their unknown but natural, shocking, gold, and they were the least of it. My skin was a lattice of scratches, which I'd known, but seeing the scores across my cheeks and forehead was vastly more dismaying than acknowledging the ones on my arms and legs. Jasper had been kind: my hair was beyond awful, an amber-colored snarl of twigs and thorns that made me look like I was half a tree. I handed Opal the mirror, and she tilted it so I could see what I was doing as I began to work the thorns out.

Jet's curious little fingers reached for the first of the thorns as I placed them aside. I snapped, "Don't touch those," and his hand flinched back. He gave me a look of tragic betrayal that would have won laughter from me, had I not been so afraid of the thorns. My gaze skittered to the window where the bit of stained glass, the leaded rose, hung, and beyond them to the roses that covered the entirety of that wall. Opal, following my gaze, shook her head. "They're the strangest roses I've ever seen, Amber. They've been growing and blooming since before they were put in the ground, but save for the branch they grew from, they have no thorns. They're not like the ones that attacked you, even if they came from the same garden."

I nodded uncertainly. Glover rose from beside Opal and got a small-necked glass jar for me to drop them in. Grateful, I smiled at him, then told the rest of my story.

Father's face grew bleaker and bleaker as I listed Eleanor's transgressions. When I finished, he shook his head, his words weary. "I knew she hadn't died."

We sisters, especially, gawked at him, and he passed a hand over his mouth, pulling at the short beard. "Not at first, for what little that may be worth. I mourned as if I'd lost a wife in childbirth, but as you grew, Amber, and played more beneath the rosebushes..." He shook his head. "Visions came to me. More than visions; memories. I *knew* I had seen you there with her, and that it was more than wishful dreaming. That little piece of knowledge shook other pieces loose, memories that couldn't have happened if she had died when you were born, until one day I saw a woman who so closely resembled Eleanor's description of the queen that I remembered she *had* claimed to have seen her. I remembered she'd said as much on the day she left us, and I think remembering it may have shattered the rest of the enchantment. I've known since then that she didn't die, and that she bore some manner of magical power."

"Why didn't you tell us?" Opal asked in astonishment. Pearl shook her head as if she anticipated Father's answer, and when it came, nodded agreement.

"What was the purpose? A mother who had died was at least not one who had abandoned you deliberately. And if she carried witchery in her blood, I thought it better to let you forget her as much as you could. I grew insular," Father admitted. "I drew you close to me and turned the world and friendships away. I wanted to protect you, but the end that was our ruin. Had I been more open, we might have had friends to turn to when our home burned, and our lives might have gone on safely in the city."

"You got out enough to meet Maman," Flint said with a quick smile. "Good thing for us, too."

Father very nearly blushed, a thing I hadn't known he could do. "Your mother sought me out. She'd known Eleanor a long time ago, in the queen's court, and heard she'd died, with children left behind. She wanted to make sure the children were well. We became friends, and fell in love. I was grateful, at the time, that anyone else cared. Now I think I may be grateful that someone, at least, counted Eleanor among their friends. It makes me feel a little less the fool."

"We became friends and fell in love," Maman agreed softly, from the stairs. "The rest…may not be precisely true."

The family turned as one to see Maman standing tall and straight on the stairway, one hand wrapped tightly around the bannister as if it lent her the strength to remain upright. She looked, to my eyes, desperately fragile: the warmth had fled from her skin, leaving it yellow beneath its mahogany hue, and she had lost weight, leaving her magnificent bone structure sharper than I'd ever seen it. She looked older, and familiar, but not in the way that a mother did to a child who hadn't seen her in a long time.

Father and I both shot to our feet, Father to offer Maman assistance on the stairs, and myself to simply stand and sway and stare. Maman gave me a rueful smile as she accepted Father's help, and the family made way for her to sit in one of the couches beside Father. I stayed on my feet, gaping at her, and it was Father who had to ask, "What part isn't true, Felicity?" in a cautious voice.

Maman looked at me, waiting to see what I knew, and after a moment I managed a whisper: "Maman is Queen Irindala."

A commotion rose, my two sisters and two of my brothers suddenly full of demands and questions. Jet, who had no questions, felt he should add to the noise, and began to wail. Glover leapt to his feet and bowed so deeply his hair swept the floor. Then he picked Jet up, trying to comfort him. Amidst all the clamor, Father ducked his head, amused guilt pulling at the corner of his lip.

"You knew," I said to him, astonished. "You *knew.*"

Maman's eyebrows went up at that accusation. "Jacob?" Her voice silenced everyone else's, and we watched them, rapt as children at the theatre.

Father lifted his gaze to hers, and my heart shattered with agony for him: his love for Maman was so clear, so obvious, and his regrets for what he had put her through written as largely on his face. "I suspected," he said. "From the beginning, I suspected."

A shadow of loss crossed Maman's features. "Is that why you married me? To wed a queen?"

"*Maman!*" Pearl burst, not, I thought, because she questioned Father's devotion, but because she had verified, with that query, that what I had said was true.

Maman arched her fingers in her lap, showing Pearl the pads, and with that minute gesture, silenced my older sister more thoroughly than she'd ever been in her life. Father, as though Pearl's outburst hadn't happened, whispered, "Of course not. I married you because I loved you. If you wanted to keep your old self secret, what right had I to unearth it? But you did look very much as Eleanor had described you, and when you said you'd once known her..." He smiled, softer and more gently than I'd ever seen. "I am sorry, Iri. Sorry for having dragged you into *this* life, when you had only asked for *that* one."

A smile twitched Maman's lips. "'Iri'?"

"Shh," Father said, primly. "It's my secret nickname for you."

Pearl threw her hands in the air as Maman, eyes sparkling with laughter, leaned in to kiss Father. Jasper, whose thoughts had flown far ahead of mine, said, "That's why you write letters all the time. You never stopped ruling the kingdom, did you? Maman, which of us is to be king after you?"

Flint, horrified, said, "Not me!" while Jet asked, "King? King?" brightly. We laughed, and Maman steepled her hands in front of her mouth before saying, "That's a concern for another time, Jasper. For now I think I must fill in the empty spaces of Amber's tale, so she can decide what to do next."

"Why didn't I recognize you?" I asked in bewilderment. "I saw you over and over in the enchantment's visions, but I saw Irindala, not Maman."

"You said it only knew the story it had experienced up until then," Maman said. "I think it only knew me as Irindala. That it had no reason to see me as someone else."

"But *I* did." I closed my eyes, recalling Eleanor's impression of the queen's face to mind. "You were younger, maybe...rounder? Softer? Your hair and your clothes were different, but...well, it's obvious *now*..."

"But you had no reason to think it, then. I was a younger woman, a long way away, in an enchanted story. It's often easier to see the lost youth in someone older, than the old woman in someone young."

I laughed as an incongruous thought struck me. "Well. I suppose Annalise will be satisfied with her references, if she asks for them. It's not often a lady's maid gets a recommendation from the queen!"

"Maman," Flint objected over my commentary, "you're not old!"

Maman gave me a wry smile, and, equally wryly, said, "I'm *very* old, my boy," to Flint. "Far older than any mortal should be. I didn't know," she admitted to me. "Until now, when you told me. I didn't know what Nell knew, that I've been leeching magic from the kingdom's very land. I'm afraid I can't maintain this artificial youth much longer without irreversibly damaging the country I fought so hard to hold." She sagged a little even as she admitted it, and I remembered she'd been bed-ridden for over a week.

As had I. I finally sat, a slow sink into cushions. "You'd better tell us everything, Maman."

"I did come to check on Nell's children," Maman said to Father, then shook her head. "No, but I must start earlier than that, when the spell to bind our borders began to fail. I knew it was my own doing. My own fault. The magic was never meant to be held by a single monarch for so long, but to be passed down from child to child, renewed by birth and love. But I had sworn to never marry again, to never carry another child until my son's curse was broken and he could kneel before me to take the crown." She smiled briefly. "I was arrogant and angry, which are bad traits in a queen. But the border began to break down, and I knew I had to do something.

"For the first years of the Border Wars I fed the land with my own blood, as I had done when I buried Euard's bones so many years earlier. It helped, but not enough. It took almost seven years of fighting before I was willing to concede that I must bear another child and give this country a future beyond me."

"*Maman!*" Flint's eyes rounded and he looked about as if he'd been caught with his finger in the sugar. "Me?"

A bittersweet smile creased Maman's features. "No, sweet. This was fifteen years or more before you were born. I couldn't bring myself to marry again, not for convenience, but there were child-makers among the men in the fields. I had a handful of affairs, and when I was certain I had caught, I retired from battle to bear the child."

"But there is no heir." Pearl spoke with a sorrowful intelligence, and for a moment Maman seemed to lean into that understanding before gathering herself to go on.

"There is no heir. The child was born too early, and never breathed outside the womb."

Opal whispered, "Oh, Maman."

Maman's smile turned bleak with thanks, then bleaker still with what she had to say. "I'll never be sure what I did was the right thing. The baby would have been my heir, had she lived, but she did not, and I had cast the spell with Euard's bones once already."

It was I who said, "Oh, *Maman*," this time, with a knot of heartbreak and pity tightening in my stomach.

She nodded, reciting the next part carefully and without emotion, as if to allow emotion would be her undoing entirely. "I returned to the field, burying her bones and saying the spell all around the kingdom, as I had done before. And for the second time, it worked.

The borders rose again, and we were safe. Safe," she repeated, with a weary laugh. "Safe, save for Nell having crossed back into the kingdom while the borders were down, and for her having born children to a man of my people."

"I didn't know," said Father, helplessly. She took his hand and squeezed it, all the acceptance and apology necessary.

"I know. Nor do I condemn you, Jacob. You might have slain her, you know." Maman closed her eyes, as if recalling the part of the story that *I* had told, how Father had stood over Eleanor's faery form and stayed his sword.

Father's chin lifted and his eyes darkened with memory. "I felt—I felt a compulsion *not* to kill that faery woman. A demand that rose from the bottom of me, as if it came up through the—"

"Through the earth," Maman said. "And spoke to you. I can't think I did it deliberately, Jacob, but even now I don't know what will happen to my oldest son if Nell dies. My fear of that unknown kept her alive that day, and what came after is therefore of my making as well. She found you, and began again. I know better than that Nell's love was intoxicating, so I can never blame you for loving her." Maman took a breath, as if steadying herself. "I only discovered her by happenstance. She was right, Amber. I'd spent decades traveling and meeting my people, without them ever knowing who I was. I wanted to see, and be seen, as a citizen, not a monarch; how else, I thought, to know the needs and wants of the people? So I was in the city, and we saw one another by chance."

"How did you disappear?" Jasper asked, fascinated.

Maman chuckled. "I'd had decades of practice by then. A cart went by while she was curtsying. I flung myself in the back amongst the rutabegas, and by the time she rose I had been carried safely around a corner. And I'm small, and had my hood up. It's easy enough not to notice me."

Father murmured, "I would disagree," and earned another sweet smile from her as she continued.

"I set someone to learn who she was, and it took little enough time, but Nell was no fool. She had fled already, and I let myself hope she had returned to the Border Kingdom. But I needed to know what I could about her children, too, and that," she said apologetically to Father, "is why I came to check on them. I was afraid I would find her greed and possessiveness embodied in them, that I would find young witches easy with using their magic to get what they wanted. Instead I found you three girls," she said, with a smile as fond for us as she'd had for Father. "You seemed to have no magic amongst you at all, but I could see the best of Nell in your mannerisms and glances and smiles. You, the four of you, showed me something of what a family could be; something I had known little off, with my campaigns and my politics and my lost child. I loved that life," she said simply and without remorse, "but I had lived it for a century, and wanted to try this other thing too. I was lucky that Jacob came to love me, as I had come to love all of you, and luckier still to have had three fine strong sons so very late in my life."

Jet, who had had more than enough of storytelling, shouted, "Maman!" and flung himself at her, snuggling ferociously before settling contentedly into her arms. Maman, murmuring over his head, said, "When the house burned and you proposed we retreat to this lodge, I was lost, Jacob. Terrified. I knew what the forest held, and I became instantly convinced that Nell had not retreated to the Border Kingdom at all. I felt in my bones that she'd come here, and I couldn't help but feel that she was drawing me back to her, determined to bring her curse to fruition at last. The forest has treated us well, but it would; it's mine. And then you found the palace, Amber, or it found you, and you chose to stay." Maman bent her head over Jet's a moment. "I dared hope that Nell had lost her strength at last, and that the curse might finally be broken, not completed.

"But then eleven nights ago I felt a terrible triumph from the wood. You've told us now what happened, Amber, but I didn't know then. All I knew was that the palace was coming under attack, and in the end, I have not lived this long to let my firstborn son go without a fight. I am sorry," she said to the rest of the family. "I know that you worry for my health, and that it's worse when I take to bed as I've done. But in many ways, this forest *is* me, and I have been fighting Nell in it these past ten days."

A long silence met Maman's final confession, until I broke it with the truth of what I'd seen: "If you hadn't, Maman, I think the Beast and I would be dead already." I described for them again the encroaching roses, and the fierce tangles of forest where the Beast had gone to stand his ground and the woods had helped him.

"'The Beast'," she murmured. "His name was Timmet, once."

A strange little pang, unexpectedly possessive, ran through me. "That was a long time ago."

She smiled at me before the smile turned to a soft laugh. "Yes, it was. And I was Irindala once, but not *so* long ago."

"Iri," Father said again, with the satisfaction

of a man who had been waiting to say it aloud for years. Maman's laughter grew and she kissed him as Jet, squished between them, let out a sleepy protest. For a moment we were together and contented, before I said, "I have to go back."

"Amber!" Opal protested, and Maman's gaze grew serious.

"It might cost you dearly, Amber."

"Maman, already, wherever I go, he is with me in spirit. Nothing can cost me as dearly as losing my Beast will."

"He's your stepbrother," Pearl said, suddenly mischievous. I gawked at her, then blushed furiously, enraged but unable to argue the fact. Maman came to my rescue, saying, "He is no blood relation to you, Amber. Pearl, be kind."

Pearl, who did not default to kindness, said, "Hnh!" and settled back, still smirking. "I'll go with you."

I shaped the word, soundless with surprise: *what*?

"At least I'm a witch, Amber. I have the pearl. And she's as much my mother as yours. More. I remember her, and you don't. There must be something I'll be able to do, but mostly I'm not letting my little sister go into battle against a faery all on her own."

"Neither," Opal said softly, "am I." She rose, smiling at our collective astonishment, and fetched the opal the Beast had sent. "I wondered, Pearl," she said as she did so. "I wondered why — if — the Beast would send you alone a gift with magical properties only you could unlock."

"They're all enchanted," I said. "Protection charms."

Opal nodded, crossing the room to the rose window, where a few small herb plants grew, and broke a leaf off a bay bush. "But a protection charm isn't the same as magic within, and he sent no instructions for Pearl. I thought perhaps I might unlock some power, if I experimented. I read the book of stones, the one the Beast replaced our lost copy of." She smiled at Father, whose eyebrows drew down in recognition, if not understanding. "Opals are reputed to have a cunning gift, if wrapped in a bay leaf and held in the hand." She held up the leaf, wrapped it around the stone, and, palming the two items together, disappeared.

Glover jolted to his feet with an anguished, "Opal!" while the rest of us shrieked in various levels of surprise. Poor little Jet began crying again, and Opal reappeared with the leaf and stone held separately again. She displayed them a second time, put them back together into her palm, and disappeared. Her laughing voice said, "I'm still here. But surely an invisible sister might be of use in your battle, Amber," before returning to our view.

Father said, "No," weakly, as if he knew he'd lost the argument before it even began. Glover said it more strongly, but with greater despair; and Pearl said, "At least Lucinda isn't here to try to talk me out of it."

"Lucinda," I echoed, far more able to grasp that than Opal's sudden resolve and magical talent. "Lucy? From the village? The one you were always sneaking off to read the cards for? When did that happen?" I considered what I'd just said, and smiled. "I suppose while you were sneaking off to read the cards."

Pearl actually smiled, and I realized once again how beautiful my oldest sister was. "Reading the cards is as nice a phrase as any."

I laughed, then extended my hands toward both my sisters. "I don't know what you can do, but I won't turn away your help. Eleanor is disembodied, but I'm not sure that doesn't make her stronger. And the longer I'm gone the more danger my Beast is in. I must go. Maman, can you send us back, through the forest?"

"I'll go with you." Maman spoke with resolve, then startled as every adult voice said, "No," firmly. "It is my battle," she said, suddenly fierce, as she had never been in all the time I'd known her. For the first time I truly saw a queen in my fragile mother, and yet I denied her with a shake of my head.

"I don't think it is, anymore. Eleanor sees me as her avatar, and the Beast has always been the piece over whom this battle is fought. This is a war for the next generation, Maman, and you have three sons to raise to princedom. Our country has no leader but you, and none of the boys are old enough to take the throne without your guidance."

"I don't *want* the throne!" Flint wailed. "I want to breed the finest line of horses this land has ever seen, with Beauty as its strong stock backbone!"

"That's all right," Jasper said. "We have an older brother who might want it anyway."

"Timmet has been long apart from the world," Maman said. "I don't know what he might want, when the curse is broken." She held my gaze a few hard seconds, studying me before nodding. "You may be right. My duty may be to my younger children, not to the oldest. But if I don't go with you, Amber, I cannot guide all of you through the forest."

"The moon rose this afternoon," Pearl said thoughtfully. "I think the pearl might make me a moonlight path. So that's one of us you don't have to send."

"A moonlight path," I said, half incredulously.

Pearl gave me a flat look. "Asks the woman who has just come from an enchanted castle housing a beastly prince?"

I breathed, "Fair point," and looked at the roses beyond the rose window. My hands began to itch. More than itch: a sting grew worse as I rubbed at my hands, and spilled into the scratches and scrapes all over my body. I reached out, and the roses visible at the window bent toward me, as if eager to feel my touch. I took a deep breath and stood. "Send Opal, Maman. I think I can get there myself."

We did not go girded for war. Had we been in the castle, we might have: the servants would have whisked armor around us, finding pieces that fit just right and required no effort to lift or move in. But despite being placed near the heart of an enchanted forest, the hunting lodge was only that, a lodge meant for ordinary people doing ordinary things: it had no armor, no swords, no shields. Just three sisters determined to do right by one another, and a worried family to leave behind. We gathered outdoors, beside the roses, for our leave-taking. I had the mirror at my hip, and removed it to hesitantly offer it to Maman and Father. "I don't know if it works here — show me the Beast, please, mirror?"

The reflective surface swirled, but rather than my Beast, I saw only roses and thorns plundering the palace gardens. They slithered like snakes, and although the mirror carried no sound, I felt like I could hear them moving, hissing against one another as they grew and explored. Maman reached out and pressed the mirror down, shutting its pictures away. "I'll need to fight with the forest, from here. If I have that to watch, I'll be too caught up in fearing for your lives. All of yours. Take it with you, Amber. Maybe it will guide you."

Opal tucked bay leaves all about her person, into her bodice, into her sleeves, even made a wreath of them for her hair. Glover, who had done so much for us, who had gotten us through our first year in the lodge and helped us thrive in our second, stood by helplessly, despair written across his features. Opal, once satisfied with her leaves, extended one hand toward him, and with the other touched the small glimmering opal necklace at her throat. "This is how I know I'll be safe," she said easily. "The Beast's opal is a thing of his palace, and for all I know, it might shatter under the pressure of enchantment there. But I carry yours with me, and its only enchantment is love. It will keep me safe." She pressed a kiss against his lips, leaving him stunned as she said, "I'm ready," to Maman, and walked confidently into the forest.

Pearl had been murmuring to her pearl for some time, a quiet discussion with it and the sliver of a daytime moon; tomorrow the moon would be new, and this venture, too late. She said no goodbyes, merely left moonlight shining under her feet.

To my surprise, the boys fell on me with hugs and tears. "You've already been gone for ages," Flint whispered. "I don't want you to go away again."

"I know, but I have to." I kissed his hair. "I'll come back, I promise."

He nodded, but looking at his face, at Jasper's—even at Maman and Father and Glover—it was clear that the only one who believed I would return was Jet, whose three years were not enough to inure him to falsehoods told to ease the heart. I hugged them all, hard, before facing the roses. Maman asked, "What will you do?" and I discovered I had to act, rather than lose my nerve by answering.

I knew they would respond to me, that they seemed to want to touch me as much as I had always wanted to touch their velvety petals as a child. It felt vulnerable, reaching for the roses —even thornless roses—with my scored arms and the blood-flecked amber that had dried on them. These roses were *my* roses, I told myself as fiercely as I could. These roses, I had paid for with my freedom, with my blood, and, I was prepared to accept, possibly with my life. They were made of my mother's faery magic, born of her rage, bent to my will, shaped by my love. I knew what could be done with roses by a true faery, and I knew what could be done with the land by a mortal woman, and I knew that somewhere between those things, an answer would be met.

They grasped me, the runners and the petals and the leaves. Not as Eleanor's roses had done, not violently, not snatching me away from the person I had come to love, but eagerly, a lover's touch in and of themselves. They ran up my arms, engulfing me, and grew up my throat and cheeks and hair. Too late, I thought that Jet, especially, shouldn't be there to see this, but I could do nothing about it now, as the rose plants writhed and wrapped themselves around my legs, fitted themselves to my groin with breathless intimacy, and wound around my torso to make a bodice of their branches. I caught a last breath, quick and shallow, and then the roses drew me in.

I lost all sense of self: I was not an *I*, but a *them*, rooted in the earth and reaching for the rain and sunshine. My roots traveled underground, finding new places to send shoots upward. I reveled in the magnificence of it, of the life that pounded through the earth, and I felt, in the distance, a darkness. A place of no life, or stunted life, and I remembered myself, and my mission.

The roses had no desire to curl in on themselves, to dive deep into the earth and race toward that dark place, but I whispered to them the truth: that there were other roses there, and that they were dying.

I didn't know how long I traveled through the soil. Far less time, certainly, than it *should* have taken a wandering rose to cut its way through miles of forest in search of an enchanted garden. I burst from the ground like a sapling unfurled all at once, shaking dirt from my hair and shoulders and gasping for air that I hadn't realized I missed.

Night had fallen while I was underground, the moon high in the sky. But then, the moon had risen in daylight anyway, and its placement was of no particular help to me in judging the time. Nor did it matter: *late* was all that mattered, and I had a fear in me that I was *too* late.

I stood before the palace gates. Their copper roses were all tarnished now, much worse than they should have been even after months of neglect, and I doubted they'd been neglected at all until the past ten days. Real roses throttled the copper ones, with pieces of metal already crumbling beneath the pressure. I stepped forward, and unlike the first time I'd encountered them, the gates did not swing open, silently welcoming. I pushed, then put my weight into it, and earned a reluctant, creaking handful of inches just enough for me to squeeze through.

Runners sprang to seize my legs. I spread one hand, hissing at them, and they backed away in angry confusion: I was clearly not meant to be able to command them, yet they were obliged to heed my wishes. It was more difficult than with my roses, and every step I took had grasping thorns tearing at my ankles.

The driveway itself was hip deep in rosebushes. They climbed the vast oak trees, working to strangle them; the oaks bent and scraped with no assistance from the wind, clearly trying to rid themselves of their attackers. I wanted to go to one, to help it fight the climbing roses, but I couldn't sacrifice everything for the sake of one tree. I whispered my sorrow, and received a sense of benediction in return: they — or Maman, conducting what she could of her own battle through the forest — forgave me for the choices I had to make.

I waded into the roses, afraid to give myself up to the plants again. There were too many of them: even breathing in their thick scent made me feel as though I was losing my sense of myself. But I went so *slowly* on foot, and I dared not ask Maman for help, not inside the palace grounds. In the forest itself, perhaps, but here, Eleanor now reigned, and I couldn't risk Irindala's kingdom for a battle I had claimed as my own. Teeth gritted against the scrape of thorns, I extended my hands. They were swollen with sap and scratches, my blood more gold than red, and they were the only way I could think extend my *power*: reaching out physically, so that I might reach out with magic as well.

To my shock, the roses parted before me.

I ran forward, relief blinding me to the possibility of a trap until suddenly the roses closed around me again, and Eleanor's floral shape emerged from the thicket. She was taller now than she'd been, and her breath fetid with decay: the weight of the roses themselves were causing them to smear together and rot. *Daughter*, she cooed again. *You have returned to make the bestial prince yours, and thus mine.*

"I've come to break your curse." The words, spoken aloud, seemed like the impotent threat of a child. All around me the roses rustled with laughter, clearly no more threatened than they would be *by* a child.

How, Eleanor wondered. *How will you, thornless Amber, break a curse that has held for a century? Even if you* could *lie with him — and how would that work*, she asked, throwing my own words back at me —*even if you could, how can you think that I would not simply destroy all of this in retaliation?*

"Maybe you will," I admitted. "But maybe you won't be able to. I intend to find out."

Or die trying! Thorn-laden branches lashed at me, scoring mark after mark and drawing blood that ran slow and thick with sap from my skin. *You don't understand*, Eleanor hissed. *The roses that waken your power are mine. The blood that they draw is mine. You tried to freeze me in amber once, little girl. Feel the power of a faery queen!*

"Are you?" I could hardly ask the question, my breath stolen from me with each bramble slash. The next time they came at me I flung my hands up, crying for them to stop, and they at least fell away for a moment. More followed, though, and I lacked the strength to stand under the onslaught. But curiosity drove me forward a step, as I tried to see whether her flowery form granted itself a crown. "*Are* you a faery queen?"

I might have been! Roses were suited to rage, with their flushed colors and heavy petals. A storm of blossoms swirled around Eleanor's unshaping form, as if anger made her lose her grip on herself. *Had Irindala not turned against me, I might have ruled her land at her side!*

I could not help a brief, sharp laugh. "I know little of faeries, Eleanor, but I think a faery queen, and a queen who is a faery, are not the same thing at all."

I paid for my humor: so many runners slashed toward me at once that I could never block them all. Still, it had been worth it, and I began to feel not just the lashing, but the *power* of the sap running within me. She had wakened me, I thought; she did not know she empowered me. I forced myself a step forward, a grin stretching my features as she struck at me again and again. I pushed away what I could, but I let as many blows land, the sap rising in me.

And then, very suddenly, I couldn't move at all, and I realized she'd known what she was doing all along, after all. She couldn't stop the blood in my veins; she needed it to be sap, so that my wounds might freeze into resin and harden into amber, as I had done to her before. Letting me struggle forward, gathering the sap in my blood, had given her enough to seize me. And *she* had had an entire garden of roses to draw from, and the full power of a faery, where I had only my own body and the half-magical blood she had granted me with at birth. *She* could escape my trap, but hers, for me, was deadly. I saw all of that in her inhuman smile, and cursed the stars for my foolishness.

But my blood was was only half of hers. I pulled that thought back, clinging to it. Unless she saturated me even further with the sap, perhaps I could hold on to my mortal aspect long enough to cast off the stiffness that had overtaken my limbs. All at once I stopped struggling, no longer straining to move myself when we both knew I couldn't. I would have collapsed, weeping, had I that much control over my limbs, but the defeat of my posture was enough: her runners withdrew to dance in the air like serpents deciding if they should strike. I gave them no reason to, my breath nothing more than broken sobs.

You see the folly of fighting a faery queen, Eleanor murmured. *You are my daughter, my only child with any love for the roses. Let me take you, little Amber. Let me fill you with my spirit, and you will know power unlike any you have ever dreamed of. You will have your Beast, and so shall I.*

A shudder ran through me; I hoped it

looked like resignation, and not revulsion. My blood, my body, my soul, were *mine* to command, not my birth mother's, and if sap ran in my veins, then sap, too, was mine to command. It was not to be crystallized inside me, but rather to flow freely, warming my skin as easily as it might bring life to a rosebush. I twitched my toes, simply to see if I could.

I could, and yet that did me no good at all, not unless I could find some way to avoid her fresh attacks; we would be here for months and years with me fighting forward a single step at a time, while my poor abandoned Beast lay far ahead of me.

I had not yet laid in any kind of plan when Pearl came stalking across the brambles on a path of moonlight, a teardrop shield of glowing pearl on one arm and a moon-bright sword in her hand.

Moonlight walked with her like a carpet, spreading across the tops of the brambles to create a shining path that cut past Eleanor and rolled on toward the palace. Her hair swept upward as if drawn to the thin moon, and I swore that her ears, too, had taken on a faery slant not unlike the Beast's. She planted herself in front of me and shouted, "Go!" as thorns lashed toward us both.

She met the attack with her moonlight

blade, severing thorns and runners alike. They fell to the ground writhing, and did not take root again. Where they landed blows against her, moonlight sparkled, taking the brunt of the hit: in one moment, when a dozen lashing branches struck her at once, I saw the shape of the enchanted armor she wore, bright and pearlescent under the moon. I backed away, breathless at what my sister had become, then scrambled onto the plane of moonlight across the roses, and ran, determined to take the space Pearl had given me.

Not only her power came to the fore: roses tried to catch me as I ran, but weaved away again as I whispered curses at them. Not curses, not like the one Eleanor had cast, but ordinary, mortal curses: *by the earth and sun and stars, stay away from me; get off, you donkey's arse; may you wither in the sun's embracing light.* The curses, breathless as they were, helped to keep me moving forward; repudiating Eleanor's work felt as powerful as the magic awakened in my veins. In that endless run, all I wanted was to be different from her, a creature of my own, worthy for being myself alone.

I hardly knew the palace grounds when I finally broke free of the avenue of roses. A barricade of forest had risen, tall and tangled as all the spots where the Beast had gone forth to try his hand against the roses. The branches parted for me and I stumbled inside them, breathless and gasping.

Wreckage met my eye. The beautifully kept pools looked like aged ruins, torn apart by Eleanor's swiftly-grown roses, and now littered with their carcasses. A ring of empty earth, appearing nearly scorched in the moonlight, lay between the new trees behind me and the palace. I stood where I was a moment, hardly believing the damage that had been wrought, then started forward again, trying to understand what I saw at the palace. Dry, dead rosebushes crackled beneath my feet as I walked, and I slowly began to understand that the palace as I knew it was no more.

It had become a writhing, squirming mass of living roses, and at its center, I could feel the faltering heartbeat of my Beast.

I broke into a run again, not knowing how I would fight my way to the castle at the heart of the enchanted kingdom, but determined that I would. I raced heedlessly up the brambles, searching for a way in, and was instead met by a fist of branches that caught me in the jaw and knocked me the long way back to earth again.

My breath left me with the impact, my whole body stunned and numb. Above me, outlined by the crescent moon, I saw thorns spiraling together into a lance, but I could not force myself to move. Behind the lance, Eleanor reshaped herself into a monstrously vast form, all roses and rage. *Did you think a little girl playing with moonlight could stop* me? she roared in my mind. *Did you think a creature as endless as roses could be* distracted *by a little sword and shield? You have chosen your lot, daughter, and you will pay for it with your —*

"Am I ordinary, Eleanor?" asked the sweetest voice I had ever known. The rose-being swung around, losing petals as it searched, but Opal was—of course—nowhere to be seen. "Such a disappointing child," she said in the most gentle mockery of a chiding tone that I had ever heard. "Perhaps that answers why I'm so biddable. Perhaps I was trying to earn the love of a mother who had no use for me."

For an instant she appeared, perfectly lovely in the moonlight. Then she cast away the aged bay leaf and wrapped her opal in a new one, in barely the time it took for her to wink at me. Her voice came again from yards away, sending Eleanor in another swirl. "Or perhaps I'm simply kind by nature, and was granted early release from a mother who might have driven it out of me. Best of all," and though her voice remained sweet as roses, acid dripped through it as well, "best of all is that in time I gained a new mother, one who did love me, and whose name I have recently learned is Irindala."

Eleanor's roar of fury was so great it carried true sound, the explosion of branches and the collapse of whole trees. The palace shook beneath that roar, falling in on itself. I swallowed a scream, knowing Opal was distracting Eleanor from me and not wanting to lose the advantage. My heart hurt, though, with terror for Opal and fear for Pearl, whose fate I could not know. My breath came back at last, and I forced myself to sit, moving as quietly as I could.

"Irindala was a good mother," Opal caroled from the safety — not that I dared think of it as such — of her invisibility. "She loved us even though we weren't her daughters by birth, and our father has never been happier than with her. Do you know, he realized you hadn't died? But he never went looking for you. Why would he? You had abandoned us, and he had earned Irindala's love. He did well, don't you think? Trading a wicked faery wife for the true love of a queen?"

Her voice danced from spot to spot, much more quickly than mere invisibility could account for. I wondered what other properties the opals had as Eleanor slammed lances of rose spirals into the earth, trying to pierce Opal's wandering voice. Opal only laughed, and I thought perhaps my kindest sister had a villainous streak after all.

Gathering courage from her mocking bravery, I plunged my hands into the palace's foliage, and became Amber in roses.

These roses did not take me kindly, as the

ones at the lodge had done. Even then I had been in danger of losing myself; Eleanor's roses wanted to tear me *from* myself. The thick cloying scent of them, tinged with rot, made my mind float outside my body, growing ever-more detached. I could feel myself gagging on the smell and had little desire to return to that sickened body. It would be easier to let go, dissolving across Eleanor's roses.

A spark of triumph shot from them, either at my own thoughts or — worse by far — at some battle won beyond the endless thicket I had entered. I snapped back into my body, dizzy again at the sickening scent of roses, and clung to the notion of sap in my veins. I offered a desperate conviction that I *belonged* with the roses, that I was not an enemy for them to spurn or destroy, and they did not listen. They rejected my presence, forbidding me to become part of them. I felt as though I retained my human shape, which I had not felt at all when I traveled beneath the earth with *my* roses. I fought for each forward step, runners and thorns digging into my shins and forehead and squeezing tightly, until I thought I couldn't possibly be moving ahead at all.

But Pearl was out there, battling roses with a sword made of moonlight, and Opal was closer still, taunting a faery monster with no protection of her own save invisibility. And the Beast lay somewhere ahead of me. If I failed, all three of them would die, and so failure could not be considered.

Things that had sap in their veins also had bark as their skin. Sometimes paper-thin bark, delicate and fragile-seeming, but even birch paper had to be peeled away in layer after layer to reach and damage the wood beneath. And I was Amber, after all: amber, which came most often from within rough-barked pine trees. If amber itself ran in my veins, surely I could convince my body that its skin was as tough as pine bark, all but impervious to the thorns. The scoring on my skin roughed it up already: I imagined those little wounds layering on top of one another like bark did, thickening like scarred wood, and bit by bit the thorns lost their bite. I kept my eyes closed, pressing forward, and finally felt brambles breaking under my feet as I regained the ability to move.

All I needed was a direction to move in, and I had no sense of that at all. The palace was enormous even when visions and memories didn't expand it beyond reality, and now it was being dismantled by the weight and fury of roses. I had entered the roses nearest, I thought, the round room that had been the library—for a moment my heart broke, thinking of all that had been reclaimed in that library, and was now lost again—and I had felt the Beast at the heart of the palace. That, to me, would always be the sitting room and adjoining hall, where Father and I had first been ushered and where the Beast and I had taken meals together. I struggled onward, but I struggled in darkness: I had no idea if I was going the right way or not, and every suspicion that the roses would force me in the wrong direction. I dragged in breath through my teeth, trying not to taste the overwhelming smell of roses, and somewhere at the back of my throat, a hint of cinnamon caught.

I froze there amongst the unforgiving roses, opening my mouth like a cat trying to find more scent. Cinnamon and myrrh, and the latter made me suddenly laugh. The roses pulled back a little at the sound, then attacked again, but in the moment they retreated, I turned toward that scent and pushed forward.

Cinnamon and sweet wine and myrrh: I had my Beast's scent, the one I had made for him, and best of all, what was myrrh but a resin? Not as hard or ancient as amber, but made from the seeping skin of trees, and thus within my demesne. Half a dozen resins were used in perfumes; I had known it without thinking it through, and now thought that Eleanor had been mistaken about us all. Even as children we three girls had played toward aspects of our unawakened magic, strengthening bonds that we would later need.

I moved faster, with the Beast's scent in my throat. The brambles grew more frenzied but less effective as I gained confidence, lashing at me, trying to tangle my feet, but also bowing to my will as I thrust them away. They scraped at my skin, but no longer pierced it: I was too much one of them, a creature of imagined bark and wood and sap. Nothing so clear as a path ever opened up, but as with the forest when I'd escaped earlier, just *enough* space cleared in front of me, and if it stitched together again behind me, that was a problem for another time.

I stepped free into what might once have been the dining hall, but which was now the eye of a bloom-laden maelstrom, rising clear to the now-moonless sky, so that all that looked down upon us were stars. I saw what Eleanor had done, how she mastered such enormous power, and I cried out in horror for my Beast.

Eleanor's roses themselves took their life from him: roots dug deep into his withered body and pinned him to the earth. The storm's eye was hardly larger than he was, just enough to let him breathe and continue to live. I did not have to be well-versed in magic to understand the wicked cleverness of what she'd done: I knew enough of Irindala, and the curse, to recognize it clearly.

Irindala was bound to the land by blood and bone and magic, and the Beast, her son, was as tied to it as she was. Through him, Eleanor could draw on the very strength of

Irindala's country, and though Maman had drained it nearly dry of magic, it still had *life* in it. To take the country's very life would nearly satisfy Eleanor, I thought. Nearly, but not quite.

But the curse lay on top of that, and curses broke laws of mortality. Eleanor had cursed the Beast to lonely immortality, and Irindala had only been able to lessen its impact. He could be made a mortal man again by a lover's willing touch...but until then even Eleanor couldn't *kill* the Beast.

She could use him, though. Any mortal creature could never have survived what the Beast now endured: the fact that he was silent, half unconscious beneath the writhing, hungry roots spoke to the pain he must have been in. But the Beast would not, could not, die, and so long as he lived, Eleanor could use his bond with the land to grow her power and wreak havoc on Irinidala's country.

Here, at the heart of her power, at the heart of his, Eleanor stepped out of the roses and I saw her true form with my own for the first time.

I had seen her repeatedly in Irindala's memories, and even through her own eyes, reflected in water, and yet she did not look like I believed her to. I had thought her tall: she was not, especially. But then, Maman was quite small indeed, and by comparison, Eleanor might be thought tall. She was rounder, too, more curvaceous than I expected; more like Opal in bosom and hip than I'd imagined.

Save for her figure, though, she was hardly like Opal at all. Opal was pretty, whereas Pearl and I were beautiful and interesting, respectively, and Eleanor was both of those things. Her features were like mine, a little asymmetrical, but the shape of her jaw and cheekbones lent her an arrogant elegance that Pearl had inherited and turned to beauty. None of us, though, shared her eyes, which were huge and angled and not at all human. Her hair was ivory, with a yellow undertone that Pearl's didn't share, and slender pointed ears poked through the straight locks. In the starlight her skin was so golden it could be mistaken for green, like the green of new growth in roses.

Her mouth curved in a deadly smile when she saw me, and the laugh that broke from her throat sounded like the scrape of thorns. "Oh, you *are* my daughter," she said in pleasure. "My foolish little Amber, throwing it all away for a Beast."

"Even if I didn't love him," I said as steadily as I could, and in a voice that didn't sound quite right, "you would need to be stopped."

"And you believe you can."

"I believe it's worth trying."

The attack came without warning, innumerable sharpened branches racing as one to pierce me. I let them, gasping as too many broke through my skin: my thoughts of bark-like protection were not, it seemed, enough to ward off killing attempts. Eleanor laughed, surprised at the ease of taking me to my knees, but I had no interest in taking her on directly. Not while she was tied to the power of the land, at least. On my knees, I was able to worm one hand through the rose roots and curl my fingers against the Beast's shin. I felt his weakening life force, and the strength of the roses, and I whispered, "No," to them.

They had bowed to my will before, parting just enough to let me pass through them. A shock trembled them now, and under my resolute command, they began to withdraw from the Beast's body. Eleanor shrieked in outrage, more and more spears raining down on me. Some struck home; more did not, as the roots pulled away from the Beast and the roses struggled to decide which of us was their master. I extended my other hand, head lowered, and thought of my thornless roses, racing now along a pathway between the hunting lodge and the palace's front gates. I called them to me, and they began to grow ever-faster. They peeled Eleanor's roses off the copper-worked gates and ran forward, moving more and more quickly as I pulled the other roots from their hold in the Beast's flesh.

He awakened screaming, a sound so terrible I wanted nothing more than to stop and comfort him. I didn't dare, knowing that if I did I would never have the chance to start again. I told myself the pain was good: it meant he was alive, and it meant Eleanor's roses were losing their grip on him.

Eleanor seized my hair, ripping my head back and slashing at my throat with nails made of thorns. They connected: I had no way to stop them. But my throat didn't slit open; it felt more like rough chunks of flesh were torn away, without any terrible pain accompanying the blows. As surprised as she was, I smiled at her. I couldn't fight her without taking my hands away from the Beast and my call to my roses; all I could do *was* smile, and so I did, confused and bright and helpless. Her eyes went mad with rage. She seized my jaw and the back of my head as a tunnel opened in her roses, *my* power bringing what it could to the fight.

It brought nothing visible, but before she could twist my head around, something struck her, knocking her away from me. My head was yanked forward as she staggered away, but my neck wasn't broken, and Opal appeared in front of me.

My sweetest sister wore a maniacal grin matched by the fierce smile on Pearl's face as she came striding down the tunnel I'd carved through the roses. They had both taken a beating: Opal limped and bled, and Pearl was scored all over by rose thorn lines. But they were neither of them defeated, and my heart soared to have them with me. As if joy fed my magic, the roots loosened from the Beast ever-faster. His screams lost strength, not as though *he* was losing strength, but as if the pain was no longer as unbearable. I cried out in relief and my sisters turned their smiles on me, then both paled and stepped back before exchanging looks and returning, resolutely, to the battle.

Eleanor made a sword of thorns and struck not at Pearl, whose moonlight armor had faded with moonset, but at Opal, whose magic was the least of all of ours. Pearl, with a sword shaped like the crescent moon itself suddenly in hand, leapt to her defense, thorn meeting pearl-drop shield. I knew from the clatter that the shield was unlikely to last long.

The final threads came loose from the Beast. Eleanor's power weakened suddenly, obviously: she staggered with the loss of it, and Opal leapt on her with driving elbows and knees, more ferocious than I had ever imagined she could be. It created the briefest lull for Pearl, who shot me a wide-eyed look that jerked to the Beast and back, as if to say *get on with it!*

I did not want to leave my sisters to fight a mad faery, but neither would the curse break if I left the Beast to help my sisters. I let the power of the roses go, surprised that the tunnel remained open, and crawled up my

Beast's body to catch his huge face in my hands. "Beast. Oh, Beast, my love, my Beast. Wake up, my love. Listen to me. Listen, beloved. Wake up, and tell me: will you sleep with me?"

Eleanor screamed. From the corner of my eye I saw Pearl's crescent sword sweep down, and light exploded all around us as the Beast transformed in my arms.

I had seen so many beasts in *my* Beast: the ram, the boar, the bear, the cat. His arching, writhing form transformed into each of them, fighting me with tooth and claw and tusk and horn. I hung on, sobbing, as he became too big, too cruel, too fierce to hold. Injuries opened on my arms, my torso, my legs: everywhere and in every way that a beast might strike in rage or fear, I was scored. I held on, afraid that if I released him I would lose him forever. Then he began to shrink, but in shrinking radiated heat, until it was as though I clung to an iron bar. A burning woody scent filled my nostrils. I screamed, but I did not let go, and suddenly the pain and the power were gone. The Beast made an ungainly *whumph* of sound as he collapsed on top of me.

He ought to have crushed me. That he did not took some consideration; the thought that we had succeeded, that the curse had ended and his transformation had been undone, took some time to reach. My heart clenched in sudden terror: I had become quite accustomed to my Beast, had fallen in love with him. I had seen the prince in a vision, but I had never thought of what he might be like, or if I would care for him. I pressed my eyes shut against the oncoming sunrise—the sky above the tunnel of crumbling roses was gold and pink and streaked with blue—and tried to tell myself that Timmet *was* the Beast, whether in an ungainly monstrous form or in his own.

A voice, his voice, but much thinner and lighter, no longer coming from a chest as broad as my arm, said, "Amber?" with much the same confusion I myself felt.

I set my teeth so I might gather my nerve, and opened my eyes to see—

—to see a Beast, albeit not the same Beast I had known, propped above me. His shoulders were no more than a man's in breadth, though like before a dark mane cascaded over them, and down his chest, like a lion's. More of a mane than before, in fact, as it had less inhuman features to struggle with, and could frame them more magnificently. His face was slim, all planes and angles softened by the loose long fur of his mane, through which the ears I had liked so much still swept upward. Like Eleanor, his eyes were huge and slanted, though his were the amber shade of a beast's, and his lips, parted in astonishment, showed teeth sharper and more deadly than any human had ever owned.

I scrambled backward, out from under him, until my back hit the brambles. It was a greater distance than I had expected: we were in a proper clearing now, and also all alone. "*Beast?*"

He sat on his heels—he was no taller than an ordinary man now, and shaped beautifully through the waist and hip, where more fur clung, offering an appealing amount of modesty to an astonishing creature. His forearms were furred as well, and his hands no longer massive paws, but slim fingers ending in unmistakable claws. He had not, I thought, looked at himself yet: his bewildered gaze was fixed on me, as though I had done something more impossible than break a faery's curse. "*Amber?*"

"It's me, Beast, I'm—oh, you can see me clearly for the first time, can't you? It's me," I repeated. "But you're—" I made a gesture, trying to encompass what had happened, trying to indicate that it had somehow gone wrong, and, catching sight of my own hand, froze.

My fingers were *branches*. Slender and knobbly with knuckles, still able to bend, but unmistakably *branches* of golden-hued wood. So were my arms, my legs; I scrambled to my feet, looking down at myself, and discovered my clothes had been torn away entirely as I'd struggled through the brambles the night before. It hardly seemed to matter: the whole of me had taken on an aspect of a living tree. Not bark-like: my torso shone more like polished heartwood, and I was dressed at hip and breast in wreathes of roses. I was warm to the touch, and the hair that fell around my face cascaded like petals, velvety against my cheeks. My toes gripped the earth like I could put down roots. My heart still beat like a woman's, fast with shock, but I was not, I realized, *afraid*. Startled, but not afraid, and, in digging my toes against the earth, I almost felt *right*, as if I had long since known where a path of roses might lead me, and had only been waiting for this moment.

Not *this* moment, though: I hadn't transformed when the Beast did. Memories flooded back: Eleanor's sharp laugh and her claim that I *was* her daughter, after all. The way my throat had not slit like a mortal's would, under Eleanor's attack, and Pearl and Opal's exchange of glances upon seeing me. I had been *other* for some little while already, although I'd been too occupied to know it. I lifted my hands to my cheeks, trying to feel if my face was at least shaped as it had been, but I wasn't' sure: I had never tried to memorize myself with my fingers before. I turned a helpless gaze at my Beast, who was no more what he had been than I was, and found him presenting a wolfish smile.

"Beauty," he said, and despite everything, I made a disparaging face.

"Beauty is our horse."

"*You* are a beauty." He came toward me, extending his hands, and then *he* saw what he had become, and stopped as short as I had, turning his palms up and down, watching the ruff of fur at his wrists fall and drape, and the light catching his deadly nails. As I had done, he spread his hands a little and looked down at himself, taking in the mane that stretched in a V down his chest, and the heavier fur at his hips. Fur grew more heavily on his calves, too, falling around his ankles very like Beauty's feathered feet, though the long clawed toes beneath it were nothing like her hooves. He looked up at me, his golden eyes wide, and I whispered, "You should see your face. It's beautiful."

He touched long fingers to his cheeks as I had done to myself, but he, who had worn a Beast's massive head for decades on end, found more changed with that touch than I had. In particular he tested the shape of his mouth, no longer overbitten from below and or weighted with tusks. He took three long strides, suddenly standing before me with a question in his eyes.

I answered it by throwing my arms around his neck and kissing him, again and again, until we were together a loving tangle of beast and botany on the earth, and the sun had risen high into the sky above us.

"So," the Beast said then, in an amused murmur against my skin, "this has not gone quite as we imagined. We may have some explaining to do."

I turned my face against his mane, inhaling his scent. Still musky, and the khemet perfume had vanished with his transformation. I would have to make more, if the ingredients could be found. I wasn't at all sure they could be: the palace had been lost to roses, and I had no idea if it would rise again. I sat up, examining the clearing as if it might hold answers.

It had grown while we were tangled in one another's arms. The sky was larger than it had been, brambles withering to dust, and some distance away, lay Eleanor's body. It had gone all to amber with roses captured inside, like some great sculptor's work. A sculptor, though, would likely have left his creation her head, and Eleanor's was missing. A thin layer of sparkling white quartz crystals glittered where her neck had been severed, as if Pearl's moonlight sword had left traces of itself behind. The moon was a barren, bright place: surely nothing slain with its light could return to life.

The head itself was gone, and a path through the collapsing brambles led away from our little clearing. Although the ground had writhed with roses when I'd noticed it last, it was now soft earth, rich and loamy and, along the pathway, marked with two sets of footprints. Quartz droplets shone against the ground, too, as if blood had fallen and crystallized. I shivered, glad my sisters had escaped and in awe of what they had done. I wondered what one did with the head of a wicked faery to quell any residual power it might have, and concluded that between them, Pearl and Maman would find an answer. I stood, and rickety branches fell in waves. Rose-scented dust lifted into the air and tinted the sky pink. I could see foundations amidst the eroding roses: something, at least, was left of the palace. Not much, but something. "I wonder what's happened to the servants."

"Gone now, with the palace. With the enchantment." The Beast—Timmet—I could not decide what to call him, even in my mind —rose and came to stand beside me.

"Were they not real?" I looked at him. "I mean, were they not transformed as you were?"

"I never thought so. I didn't know any of them from their behaviors or opinions, as I'd known my own servants. I think everything here was made of Nell's magic. Everything except me, and I was shaped by it. Everything except you."

"I was *born* of it," I said a little dryly. More

than a little, perhaps: my voice had altered somewhat to my own ears, both deeper and more rustling, as if the creak of an old tree spoke along with the whispers of wind in its leaves. It lent a depth to my asperity that hadn't been there before. I thought Pearl would like it.

The Beast, whether he liked it or not, at least chuckled. "There is that. So nothing here is... real."

"Or everything is, and ever was. I think I can..." I extended a hand, calling life from the exhausted and dying roses around us. One single runner came to me, climbing into the air to offer me an amber-tinted thornless bloom. I offered it to the Beast. He took it gingerly, but his golden gaze remained on me.

"What has happened to you, Amber? This was never part of the curse."

"This is the price of wakening faery blood to save a prince." I flexed my toes in the soft earth, feeling it accept me in a way it had never done when I wore human skin. "I didn't know this would happen, but I wouldn't undo it. I don't feel much different. A little stronger, maybe. I'll have to figure out how to brush my hair, and whether sitting in a bath will ruin my finish."

The Beast laughed with surprised. I grinned back at him, then turned my attention to the failing brambles. "I feel as though I can call green things to me. Not just the roses, but everything, I think. The earth is...hungry. Needy. Not just here, but throughout Irindala's country. I think I can feed it. I think I *have* to. If you and I are born, in our own ways, of enchantment, then..." A breath escaped me and I opened my hands to encompass the ruins we stood in. "Then maybe this is only enchantment in need of caring, just as all of Irindala's country needs care. I hate to lose it, after all of this. I feel as though I have a duty to it. Your mother warned me there would be a price for breaking a curse so old and heavily weighed on the land. Perhaps this is it."

"My mother?" The Beast turned to me with a graceful movement, lithe and very unlike the Beast he had been, but also familiar in its power. "You've seen my mother?"

"I—oh." I reached for his hand. "Your mother is my Maman, my stepmother. I didn't know until yesterday." I glanced uncertainly at the sky, with its rose-colored sun, then back at the Beast. "If it was yesterday. When I left you, whenever that was."

I had learned to read the Beast's expressions well, and Timmet's were far easier *to* read, for all their still-inhuman cast. He blinked slowly, clearly nonplussed. I curled my arms around him and breathed his scent again before chuckling. "We will have a *great* deal of explaining to do, not just to our family, but each other. Beast—Timmet—"

He exhaled, a curiously small sound. "I

haven't heard that name in a very long time. I wonder if it fits me anymore."

"It does," I said with brash confidence, and then, more softly, "but so does 'Beast', and so might something else entirely, if you prefer it. I don't understand what went wrong, my love. I thought you would be brought back to yourself. I'm afraid—I'm afraid I did this to you somehow. Because I loved the Beast. And because I'm—" I looked down at myself, then back at my Beast.

"Mmmn." He shook his head. "What is 'myself'? I was human for eighteen years and a beast for over a century. Anyone might change in that time, even so much that they no longer knew the mortal form they once wore." He extended a clawed hand, so much more human than it had once been, yet still so animalistic. "I think you could not have done this to me, no matter how changed *you* are. Not alone, at least. If I were not content to be some of one and some of the other, I think no matter how much you loved the Beast, I would have become what I once was. But the Beast is my most familiar form, and I feel connected to it still." A smile, much more clearly a smile than that which his more beastly face had expressed, curved his lips. "Connected, but much less lumberous."

"I believe I'm the one who is now lumberous," I said with a brush of branch-like fingers, and earned a withering look worthy of Pearl, had it not also been laced with amusement. Smiling in return, I said, "Pearl and Opal will tell Maman and Father that we're all right, but we should probably go to them. Maman has waited so long to see you again. And we should figure out where a living tree and a beautiful beast belong in this world."

"Together," the Beast said softly. "We will never, ever be apart."

"Together," I agreed, and then because I could not help it, I added, "except perhaps when we require the necessary. Or I wish to have a gossip with my sisters, or you a wrassle with your brothers, who will be most taken with your extraordinary form. Or—"

"Enough!" Timmet roared, and if he lacked the volume he once had, it was easier to hear the humor in his voice. We laughed together until the tears came, and I thought us the better for it.

I took his hand in mine, and together we went to see what the world would make of us.

Acknowledgements

Beauty and the Beast has always been my favourite fairy tale. My Negotiator Trilogy (*Heart of Stone*, *House of Cards* & *Hands of Flame*) is a shout-out to it, but a not-so-secret part of me always wanted to write a Proper Version of the tale. I recently discovered I hadn't, after all, read the oldest extant written version, which proved to be by French novelist Gabrielle-Suzanne Barbot de Villeneuve, and was written in 1740, almost twenty years before the better-known adaptation written by Jeanne-Marie Leprince de Beaumont. There were wonderful elements in de Villeneuve's book that had been excised by de Beaumont, and I knew I'd finally found the basis I wanted to build my own *Beauty and the Beast* story on. Writing it was a joy, and I hope you've gotten as much pleasure from reading it as I did from writing it.

I'm *exceedingly* grateful to Tara O'Shea, who turned the cover art around in record time, as well as to my father, Tom Murphy, editor-and-copy-editor extraordinare, and to Catherine Sharp, Sherilyn Petterson, Ruth Long and Alethea Kontis, all of whom have shown great support for this book. You're all my heroes.

Finally, but not at all least-ly (look, I'm an author, I can make up terrible words if I want to), all my love to my husband and son, who keep me going when things get tough.